TO BE READ AS DAY TURNS TO NIGHT

Stephen Rawlinson

Contents

Foreword

When I was in the Scouts, we used to tell each other scary stories, as children often do. Sometimes we would be huddled in our sleeping bags inside our tent late at night, pretending to be asleep, so as not to get caught by the disapproving leaders; at other times we would be gathered around the campfire, sitting in a circle under the stars, enjoying toasted marshmallows and hot chocolate, keeping ourselves safe and warm.

The teller of the story would usually have a mag-lite torch as a major prop, switching it on and then pointing it upwards, so that the beam highlighted their face, giving off a somewhat spooky effect.

And then, once all were settled, we would hear (the teller putting on an intimidating voice to sound like some kind of demonic narrator) stories of monsters in the bushes, ghosts, witches and other abominable creatures which would be out to get us when we least expected it, impressing upon us that at night, campsites could be dark, lonely, isolated places, and full of horrors for vulnerable young Scouts.

Some of the stories were dreadful, but others were so good, that we would later find it difficult to sleep, lying awake in the darkness of the night, hearing every howling, every hooting, every footstep, and every twig cracking, wondering if the thing we had been told of earlier that evening, was lurking outside, with us as its intended prey.

In later years, I decided to continue the tradition of telling ghost stories, albeit in written form. As the editor of the Scout troop's newsletter, I decided that it would be 'fun' to write a ghost story for Christmas, my first being The Crooked Finger of Doom, in 2009 (which I have recently returned to, re-edited and expanded for this collection), and this was then followed by more.

To begin with, the stories were intended to be little more than entries for the newsletter and an 'entertaining terror' if you like, something that would be quick and easy to read on a side of A4 paper. As they became popular and I grew more confident, I began to write longer stories, with a broader range of settings, eventually moving away from Scouting themes and focusing on my workplaces, as well as places I had visited on day trips, and on my travels, amongst other things, sharing them with friends, family and colleagues.

Now, however, having returned to them, I feel that the time has come to share some of my stories with a wider audience, so that I can warn of the supernatural perils that await us if we tread where perhaps we should not, or stray from the warmth and safety of the campfire.

Strange things do indeed lurk out there, as you shall soon discover...

It was clear that apart from him, not one of them there was alive!

PART ONE

*Ghost Stories From Around
the Campfire*

The Crooked
Finger of Doom

An account of what happened to an unnamed Scout troop

It wasn't the most pleasant of evenings as it was cold, wet, and horrible, but this didn't stop them from going to their weekly Scout meeting inside their hall. It was a shabby little place, in all honesty, where the roof leaked regularly, and the walls - despite many of them having been rebuilt and re-plastered not long previously - were already in need of attention and offered little in the way of insulation due to cracks and crumbliness. It also wasn't the cleanest of places, despite the best efforts of everyone to make it so; as a result it was full of cobwebs, and plenty of spiders lurked just about everywhere - large ones too in some places - whilst there was also a slightly unpleasant musty smell, as well as a dusty wooden floor (which meant that the children often went home in need of a shower and their uniforms a good wash, especially if they had been rather active in games or other activities, and had been on the floor at any time).

The Troop were going to spend more than the usual couple of hours there as, after the meeting, they were going to have a sleepover inside, to raise money for a new mini-bus - the one they currently had was rather elderly and becoming unreliable - but it could be argued, that the attention of the fundraising may well have been put to better use on the hall itself, and I think, as such, it would be fair to establish that this wasn't the most hospitable of venues at the best of times, with the Scout Group rather strapped for cash, and so as far as some of the children were concerned, it may not have been place-of-choice for a sleepover.

The meeting itself had been uneventful: it had begun with a game of hockey, followed by badge-work - which, this week, was first aid and map reading skills - with a game called Hot Rice to finish off. Hot Rice was one of those games where, as mentioned, the Scouts would be highly active; the older, Explorer Scouts were in charge of running the game, and it was their job to throw a football at the rest of the Scouts and try to hit them below the knee, whilst the Scouts ran around and did everything they could to avoid being hit, and some of them did end up on the floor as a result. The whole point of the game, from the Leaders' perspective was to tire the Scouts out, so that it could be as peaceful a night as possible.

Once the regular meeting had finished, the Troop settled down to some nibbles from the troop's tuck shop and sat in a circle as if on camp and sitting around the campfire. Within the circle which they had set up, the Scouts talked amongst themselves, but one of the older, Explorer Scouts, a girl of 14, who had a tomboy-ish nature and an air of authority about her, suggested in a loud voice that they could tell jokes, mind teasers, or stories. As no one had anything to offer, she began with a mind teaser which proved to be rather challenging, and indeed, frustrating for the struggling listeners who were trying to figure out the solution, which as it turned out, was simple and obvious, as they often are when thinking about them in hindsight. She then tried another, but soon, mind teasers became tedious and boring, and so some of the Scouts told jokes, some of which were successful, others not so. With the Leaders pre-occupied with other tasks, it seemed that this particular Explorer was dominating proceedings, like some kind of ringmaster or chairperson of an event. With the mind-teasers and jokes having been exhausted, she decided to alter the ambience of the evening, and, as if pre-planned, she got up and went over to the collection of switches which controlled the lighting in the hall.

"What are you doing?" enquired the main Leader, in a tone which hinted at disapproval, as some of the hall lights had been turned off.

"Creating a ghost story atmosphere" was the confident reply from the Explorer, as she sat back down again within the circle.

"Well, keep it short, it's time for bed soon" the Leader said, checking his watch, anxious that the Scouts would find it difficult to sleep on the hard floor anyway, even without the added extra of the great noise of the wind which had begun to howl outside. Telling ghost stories, he thought, may well add to any sleeping problems by leading to nightmares, especially if the Scouts stayed up far too late.

"Ok, ok", the Explorer said, with an air of protest and determination not to adhere. She had with no intention of going to sleep any time soon, and she knew that with a ghost story, she would have a captive audience who she could manipulate and encourage to be on her side in the matter of staying up as late as possible.

"I'll tell you of what happened here on this site, many years ago, before the hall was built......." she began, mischievously, grabbing hold of a large Mag-lite torch, switching it on in the near-darkness and shining the beam upwards towards her chin, to create an added, terrifying effect. The rest of the Scouts hushed and listened intently as she lowered her voice.

The story which she told them is a fairly well known one around the locality, and is included below, albeit in my words, not hers:

The official verdict on 'The Blue Death', as the newspapers called it, was murder. The wife of the murdered man was, despite heavy protestations, convicted and sentenced. The motive, it was claimed, was that she had been jealous of an affair he had been having with one of her friends, although there was no actual evidence of any such affair. The method of murder was under some dispute, as it was not clear whether the man had been poisoned, or his skin had been painted so that it suffocated due to a lack of oxygen. One thing was clear, however: Mr Fairfax had been found in the middle of the night, lying in his bed, quite dead, and his body a bright blue colour.

The locals have always known that the lady in question was innocent and an easy scapegoat, but at the time of the investigation, their claims and theories were rejected by the authorities for being too fantastical. This had not been the first such death, and in fact, they had been occurring for decades, but although it was always claimed officially that the victims had died because of copycat murders, following on from the very first incident, locals know that this was most certainly not the case.

The event referred to at the opening of this story took place in 1926; back then there was a manor house on the land (it has since been demolished and the grounds used for other purposes: flats, a school, Scout headquarters etc). The house had had several different owners over the previous few decades, and it did have a reputation of death: there had been similar cases of the mysterious 'Blue Death' over the years which, as has been said, had been treated as copycat murders. But the house itself was splendid; built in the late 1770's as a replacement for an earlier building, and was perched on top of a small hill, with some nice, if small, gardens, as well as a good view out at the back.

Herbert and Maxine, a young, trendy couple (he was very dapper, and she was an archetypal flapper girl) had purchased the house and brought with them a small number of staff to help run it. They were planning a drinks party and had invited a few friends, including Mr and Mrs Fairfax, down from London to join them. The preparations for the party went remarkably well, although there was one rather curious episode beforehand.

One of the maids first noticed it one morning, sitting there, outside the door through which the servants entered the kitchen from the back of the house: it was a large toad, grey and slimy, with piercing eyes - red, she thought - which glared at her, as if watching her every move. It became something of a regular visitor and would sit there each day, observing the movements of the staff, and one day, it even had the boldness to not only jump up to the kitchen windowsill, but then to try and cross the threshold through the open window and gain entry to the house. It didn't get very far before being ushered back out by the startled cook, who, it was later discovered, had burnt her hand. It was a painful, smouldering burn which simply wouldn't heal, forcing her to leave her position, as she was unable to continue her work. The locals believed that it was her touching the toad to remove it which was the cause of her dreadful injury.

The party itself was a great success, with the attendees drinking lots of champagne and cocktails, and eating lots of delicious food. Guests were in fancy dress, with the hosts as Anthony and Cleopatra and Mr Fairfax as a harlequin. Everyone chatted, laughed, played games such as charades, and danced to jazz music played on the gramophone. However, it was during the night that terror unfolded.

Everybody had turned in late, and where possible, couples had been put up in the same bedrooms. The Fairfaxes had their own room at the far end of the Eastern side of the house, which was nearest to the local church. The testimony of Mrs Fairfax, who was convicted of her husband's murder, was never revealed to those outside of the official investigation, but the vicar who came to visit her in jail did pass on to some of the locals what she had told him, as it tallied with their own thoughts and suspicions on the matter.

According to Mrs Fairfax, they had gone to bed sometime in the early hours, but they had been partying and drinking so much that she did not know at what time. Her husband had been completely fit and healthy, falling asleep quite normally. During the middle of the night, Mrs Fairfax was woken by what appeared to be music playing. It was faint at first, as if coming from some distance away, but as she listened, and the sound became louder, she realised that it was organ music, and upon listening further, she recognised it to be Toccata (and Fugue in D minor) by Bach. The temperature in the room had dropped, but what chilled her the most was that the music seemed to be being played live, despite the fact there was no organ in the house. Suddenly there was a flash of lightning, followed by a crack of thunder as the rain pounded on the window. Then there was another flash. This time the crash of thunder was simultaneous with the lightning, and she saw, in a shadow made by the terrific flash of light, a finger, long and crooked, rising above them. It moved, slowly and menacingly downwards towards her husband who was lying beside her. She screamed and switched on the electric light beside the bed and saw that there was nobody else in the room but them. Then, she screamed again with horror as she saw her husband lying there on the bed, his body bright blue and lifeless, his skin burning to touch.

Mrs Fairfax's screams had awoken the rest of the house, and as the hosts, staff and other guests entered the room, they all saw the horrifying sight; however, there had, of course, been no other witnesses to what had happened. The police were called in to investigate, and the press also became interested in the case, and whilst it seems that alcohol and conventional drugs were ruled out as possible causes of death, Mrs Fairfax, having been the only other person present at the time of death, was accused of murder, most likely as a convenient way of bringing the case to a close as quickly as possible, and preventing any 'wild' and 'irrational' speculations. It was noted, however, that she had sustained burns to her hand which, apparently, refused to heal.

Upon hearing of the events at the house, the locals knew it to once again be the work of Mrs Heversome, who had been tried and then hanged as a witch some centuries before, her body buried away from the nearby church and graveyard in a spot marked by nothing more than a small stump. She had lived near to the site of the manor house in a tiny dwelling and had been accused of malevolent sorcery born out of jealousy – something to do with being spurned by whoever it was who had been in residence on the site at the time - with one of her curses apparently involving killing a person by turning them blue. It was said that she had kept a few animals, one of which had been a large grey toad, which many suspected to have been her familiar (evil in animal form, acting out her wicked deeds either on her behalf, or as herself transformed). After her death, there had been 'unusual' sightings, but none which could be attributed to anyone or anything specifically, and before long the deaths began, and these followed the same pattern as already described. Despite her own death, they were attributed to her, as if she still lingered around the site somehow.

It is said that in Victorian times, a cult following developed, involving the owners of the manor house at the time and some of their friends. They had heard of Mrs Heversome, and the talk of locals regarding her, and had become fascinated by the story, and as many did in the latter years of the 19th century, they tried to summon her restless spirit. After some experimentation, they determined that the most effective way of summoning her was using music, but, as often happens when people meddle in things they do not understand fully, it seemed that by summoning her spirit, they unleashed her hatred and her need for revenge on those who occupied the site, quickly losing control of her. So taken by these stories and events were they, that subsequently, over the years, different owners banned musical instruments in the house in an attempt to stop the occurrences, but by 1926 you didn't need instruments to play music, as a gramophone would suffice, and it would not need a huge leap of imagination to believe that it could have been forced to play music by itself through some kind of 'power', even if the music in question (i.e. Bach) was not on among the record collection.

Herbert and Maxine, so distressed by the whole affair, abandoned the place, and before any new owners arrived, some of the locals carved daisy wheel symbols by various entrance points around the house in an attempt to prevent Mrs Heversome from gaining entrance to the building in any shape or form again. Why it had not been done before is unclear. Some of them also took it upon themselves to exhume her, but upon digging at her burial site - which, it should be noted, was discovered to be on the edge of the manor house's grounds and had not been disturbed - they found no body at all, only smouldering scorch marks suggesting where her body had been but was no longer.

"Mrs Heversome's body was never found, but over the next 70-80 years the manor house was replaced and there were more sightings of the crooked finger, accompanied by the organ music, and of course, the Blue Death" the Explorer announced, before concluding "and who knows when she may strike again!" to gasps from several of the Scouts.

"Where did you get that from?" asked one of the Leaders, who had been listening to the story, despite initially being dis-interested in the idea of ghost stories.

"I dunno, I just heard it from someone in my Explorer unit, and he told me that he reckons that it's the ghost of Mrs Heversome who has the crooked finger, and that her 'power' became such that she herself was able to make the music which summons her".

"Has anyone else got any good ghost stories?" a Scout asked, excitedly.

"No, it's time for bed" said the main Leader, getting up out of his chair, much to the disappointment of several of the Scouts, and eventually, amid protests, the Scouts and Explorers finally admitted defeat. The hall was briefly relit as they dispersed from the circle, and laid out their sleeping arrangements, which were typically sleeping bags with foam roll-mats underneath, while there were also a small number of foldable camp beds in place too. It certainly wasn't the cosiest or snuggest of locations on a wild and wet autumnal night, and the cold, hard flooring was unforgiving and not at all comfortable, all of which made sleep much more difficult to attain, especially with some of the Scouts still excitable after the evening which they had had, the stories which had been told, and the opportunity of being with their friends and away from parents for the night.

Eventually, sleep came to them, whilst outside, the rain lashed down and the wind continued to howl, with the leaders probably having good reason to be concerned that they would awaken in the morning to find the roof had leaked. The hall had certainly had its problems with a leaky roof before, and it was an area of great concern with regards to the building's redevelopment and ongoing maintenance and repairs, and of course it was just typical that they had picked such a foul night as this in which to hold a sleepover, the irony perhaps not being lost on anyone in attendance.

The Explorer Scout, the girl whose story had become the main centre-piece of the evening, found it difficult to sleep, but she wasn't the only one and at one point, deeper on into the night, she heard movement, in the form of rustling, followed by light footsteps. She opened her eyes and saw that it was one of the younger Scouts who had risen from out of their sleeping bag, and gingerly made their way towards the toilet, in the dark, trying desperately not to step on anyone as they went. The Explorer watched them carefully, as they safely navigated their way to the toilet, switched on the light, and within a few minutes, returned the way they had come and settled down again. As they did so, she asked them, in a whispering voice, if they were OK, and they affirmed in reply that they were.

There was a flash of lightning and then a crackle of thunder, loud enough to be heard with significance over the din of the heavy rainfall upon the roof. As the rumbling of the thunder faded, another sound emerged, subtle at first, and one which seemed to be coming from some distance away. The Explorer didn't notice it to begin with - and to be fair, it would probably have needed her to be concentrating and straining her hearing to have detected it straight away - but it was there, nevertheless, and upon being alerted to it, she found that it seemed to be getting ever so slightly louder and clearer, as if it were approaching from somewhere.

As it became more audible, she realised that it was the sound of classical music, being played on an organ. She listened intently. Electronic devices such as i-Phones had been banned from the sleepover, and unless one of the Scouts had disobeyed the instruction and was playing music on their device, she was unsure where the music could be coming from.

"Are you still awake?" she whispered through the dark - with a touch of nervousness as well as annoyance - in the general direction of the Scout who had recently visited the toilet.

"Yes" was the reply.

"Have you got your i-Phone on you?" was the next question.

"No" the Scout replied. The pair of them stopped whispering, and yet the faint music still played and continued to become ever so slightly louder and seemingly, closer to them.

"Where's that music coming from?" whispered the Scout, now becoming rather anxious. The Explorer contemplated her response, trying to think rationally, but before replying, the Scout continued, in a tone which suggested that fear was beginning to envelope them.

"It's just like in the ghost....."

"It's just a story" came the complacent interruption – which belied the fact that she too was unsettled - from the Explorer, attempting to deny the possibility that the Scout's wild suggestion was no longer implausible. As she continued to listen, a chill ran through her. Her senses were now as alert as they had ever been, as the music continued and kept on increasing in volume and lessening in the distance it seemed to be from them, the pace at which it did so now quickening at an increasingly alarming rate.

"What's that noise?" whispered the voice of another Scout, who had been woken up, followed by another.

"It's the ghost" answered the first Scout who was now very much distressed and had sat up straight in their sleeping bag.

As the waking Scouts now started to murmur, the music kept on increasing in volume, going up and up and up all the time, the intensity building every second, up to the moment when it seemed that it was now there with them, reverberating all around them, seemingly in readiness for a terrible crescendo to come!

And then, suddenly, there was another flash of lightning, an almighty crack of thunder, and a sickening scream, as rising up from the darkness was seen the shadow of a crooked finger, its size enhanced by the sudden stream of light.

Moments later the hall lights were turned on and the entire Troop began to wake up. The Scout, who had only minutes earlier paid a visit to the toilet, unaware and unprepared for anything resembling menace to come, was palpitating, finding it hard to breath as the shock of what they had seen and heard hit them, as hard as their scream had hit the others as they had slept. Several members of the Troop rushed over to tend to the Scout and try to calm them, realising at once that they had witnessed something quite appalling and had screamed to alert everyone to the event which had occurred.

For the other members of the Troop, there was someone else who required attention, although it soon became obvious that there was nothing that could be done, because there, lying in her sleeping bag, was the Explorer Scout. She was dead, and her skin the colour of bright blue. Despite wanting to, nobody dared to touch the body, as they now knew the story of the 'Blue Death', the teller of it now having become the latest victim.

The Wrong Tent

The Scout leaders had decided that despite the advice from the concerned campsite manager, site 13 was perfect; it was grassy, mostly flat, reasonably sized and surrounded by woodland, with some of the site set in amongst the trees and nettled bushes. The fussy, elderly manager, who had given the impression of having worked and even lived on the campsite for some years, had commented, without offering any expansion on his words, that the site was 'disused', and although it did seem a little overgrown in places - having presumably been an even bigger site in years past – it seemed fine.

Initially the troop had been allocated the neighbouring site, number 14, and although you may think that it would be just next door, as such, the size of the campsite overall meant that individual sites were well spaced out from each other, with each being its own clearing in the woodland and connected by a network of tracks just large enough to fit a minibus and accompanying trailer, albeit with very little breathing space.

Unfortunately, upon inspection, it was decided that site 14 just wouldn't do. For a start, it was smaller than the troop required, and the slightly hard and uneven terrain would not be accommodating for their purposes. Bartering then ensued and despite his protestations, the manager eventually relented and reluctantly agreed that they could take a look at site 13, and as already mentioned, the leaders were far happier with it and elected to take it instead.

The manager had been adamant that it would not be suitable and began some sort of rambling monologue which he directed at them, but due to his slightly nervous and panicked disposition, it came across as rather incomprehensible. Eventually he walked away, wearing the look of a defeated man who had pleaded all he could with those who, he felt, had been overtaken by their own ignorance, and retreated, still mumbling to himself in some disgust.

"I can't see what he was going on about" said the Group Scout Leader in the aftermath of this interaction, as he was walking around the site with the other leaders, "there's nothing wrong with it".

"Something about it not being used since something or other - I'm not really quite sure what he was saying as I couldn't make him out, the silly old fool" said another, as the four leaders circled round their prize with an air of unnecessary smugness, none the wiser as to why the manager had reacted with an air of panic.

The troop were staying for five nights during the October half term and the weather was cold but crisp for the time of year and it would be ideal for an Autumn's camp. There were 15 Scouts attending, all between the ages of roughly 10-14, and they would be sleeping and cooking in three separate patrols, hence the necessity for a larger sized site. Upon parking the minibus and trailer at the edge of the site, the entire troop came together to unload the trailer's contents, and from it came a large amount of equipment such as: tents, dining shelters, gas stoves and cannisters, wooden tables and benches, cooking utensils, axes and bow saws – in fact the list of items being transported would seem endless if one were to be watching from afar, half-expecting the kitchen sink to appear at some stage as well.

After the unloading of equipment came the setting up of the camp, and in this, the Scouts worked well, with each patrol pitching their own tents and dining areas. While many Scout troops used more modern tents, the troop in question favoured a more traditional approach, using 'double four' tents. These were made from thick, heavy duty green canvas, with wooden poles for support, thick guy ropes, and large wooden pegs used to secure the tent to the ground. But whilst most of the troop were hard at work that afternoon, there was one member who was, in fact, quite the opposite.

Harry was a small boy, probably slightly below average in height for his age, and was what you might call a 'cheeky-chappy', in that in one instant he would come across as all sweet and innocent, perfectly capable of putting on a dow-eyed expression, while in another he would have a devious smile indicating that he was plotting or undertaking some sort of mischief. It could certainly be said that he was something of a handful for the adults and indeed the more senior Scouts, such as his Patrol Leader, and as he often liked to do his own thing, he could be something of a loner, with few other friends within the troop.

"Harry!" his Patrol Leader shouted in frustration for a second time in as many minutes, "help us out here rather than just standing there and staring". Harry had been standing a few metres away from the rest of the patrol, at first vaguely swinging a wooden mallet at nothing in particular, looking distracted, and then staring off into the woods, whilst the rest of the troop had been working on erecting their tents.

On hearing his name at the second time of being called, he turned around slowly, weakly responding.

"I was just wondering who those two kids were" he said, looking back towards the woods. As he did so, he blinked in an exaggerated manner, as he could no longer see anyone there.

"Just some other Scouts" the Patrol Leader assured him halfheartedly and somewhat dismissively, but Harry wasn't convinced. Although they had only appeared vaguely to him from the shaded woods – standing there as a group of four, watching him –

he certainly didn't recognise them as other members of the troop, and besides, the rest of the troop was hard at work and had no need to be in the woods just yet. He felt that there was something odd about them and that they were different somehow to most other Scouts he had encountered. After another rebuke from his Patrol Leader, Harry rejoined the others in tent pitching, before dinner needed to be prepared.

That evening, after dinner, the Scouts had a wide game of Smugglers. It was a game which saw the troop split into two, with half of the troop sent on the run, as it were, with a small, sealed gas cannister wrapped in toil foil (the pretence being that it was a nuclear cannister), which they needed to return to the centre of the site – called basecamp - avoiding capture from the other half of the troop, whose mission it was to give chase and claim the cannister before it could be successfully returned. Harry was part of the running team and was given the task of hiding the cannister for a brief time, before it would be recovered, when safe, by another team member to return it to base. After walking for a good 10 minutes through the campsite - and by this time it was becoming very dark and some of the paths were moist and poorly lit - he found himself at the shower block, which although well lit, was a grim, uninviting place, as campsite facilities often are. It had been decided in advance that the shower block would be used as a place to hide the cannister, and Harry felt glad that he had reached it safely and would be able to dispense of it.

As he approached out of the darkness, he understood from looking around him, that he appeared to be alone, and yet, he heard a voice. Although he couldn't necessarily make out who had spoken, he heard it plainly and distinctly, amid the calm and gentle air. His first thought was that of panic, because it occurred to him that he had already been discovered by his opponents, and so he made it his priority to get inside and hide as soon as possible. But then, before he could enact his plan, he felt someone brush against him from behind, and spinning around, expecting see one of the chasing team, he saw instead the retreating figure of a Scout, but not one that he recognised. He knew that it was a Scout because he saw, from the brief glimpse that he had of them, that they were in uniform, and his Patrol Leader's words about there being Scouts present from other troops re-entered his mind. But his instincts told him that there was something else, something different about this Scout, who had darted to the corner of the block, giggling. Harry gave chase and having rounded the corner, caught another glimpse of the figure. Their uniform was not like his, or indeed any other that he had seen, and although not too dissimilar, he saw that it seemed to feature a different shade of green to his own, and that the Scout was wearing a beret and shorts (which seemed most inappropriate in a cold October half term). Harry tried to call out to them, but before he could muster a call of any great sound quality, the Scout had again disappeared, seemingly having gone off, deep into the woods. After a few moments contemplating what he had seen and felt, and now confused but also curious, Harry felt another brush against him, but this time he did recognise the person responsible, as it was one of the chasing team and he had been caught. The game was over.

Harry protested as he was given the blame for his team's failure in the game, a failure which was compounded when the teams swapped roles, and the other team was successful in returning to basecamp with the cannister. He was adamant that he had seen, for a second time, one of the 'other' Scouts, who he had initially seen earlier that day, staring at him from within the woods. If they were from another troop, as his Patrol Leader suggested, then perhaps he could make friends of them, and this was something that he decided he would attempt to do. But the uniform he saw the Scout wearing was, subconsciously, proving to be something of a sticking point, as he couldn't get over how different it was, and it introduced an element of caution to his plan to approach them and any others in that troop and become friends.

That night, Harry slept reasonably well to begin with, but was woken around 2am by a sharp clap of thunder and the sound of rain on the roof of the tent. It also seemed to be rather gusty outside, as he could hear the wind too. He lay there, in his sleeping bag, for about half an hour trying to get back to sleep, but eventually he gave up and decided to have a look outside. The tent, being elderly and of another era, did not feature a built-in groundsheet, or doors which you could simply unzip; you had to manually untie the door flaps and then unhook them from the wooden pegs at the base of the upright pole. In the dark, it could be an arduous task to escape the tent, and after some frustrating minutes, Harry was able to open the doors as much as was necessary - and indeed possible - and peered outside. Strangely, all was calm. The ground was damp, but not wet or muddy as you might have thought, and the sky was cloudless. There was an eeriness about the outside air, which was moist and chilly, with mist beginning to descend. But there was certainly no sign of anything untoward, and aside from the sound of a gentle breeze, or an owl in the distance, there was very little to disturb a good night's sleep: certainly no rain, thunder or gale. Surprised, Harry closed the tent, got back into his sleeping bag and went back to sleep, too tired to allow the absence outside of what he had expected to find, disrupt him further.

The next morning was cool, foggy and damp. Harry asked the rest of the troop if they had heard the storm the previous night, and as it turned out, no one had, although his Patrol Leader mentioned that he had been woken by rustling around the tent, as if an animal had been trying to get in. After breakfast, Harry, feeling rather workshy, as per the reputation he had built within the troop, skipped cleaning and washing up, and made his way up to the providore, the campsite shop, which sold essentials, sweets and chocolates, and also souvenirs. In his defence, one could argue that Harry was not only independent, but also inquisitive, hence his tendency to wander off by himself, even if he tended to do it when it should have been time to work. Outside the providore - which was located near towards the top of the campsite and by its entrance - was a vending machine, and it was here which Harry intended to go to, as he wanted to pick up a bottle of fizzy drink. But as he approached, he was disappointed to find that another Scout was there, standing in front of it, and if he wanted something, he would have to wait his turn. It was a much brighter morning here, with the fog which seemed to plague his troop's own site not prevalent, and on a second glance, he noticed that the Scout was not really doing anything, but was just standing in front of the machine, seemingly motionless. From what he could make out, Harry believed that it was one of the Scouts with the strange uniforms, and if that were indeed the case, it would be the perfect opportunity to make friends. In his determination, he quickened his pace towards the machine, noting that the Scout had now, it seemed, turned towards him.

Harry's eyes fixed upon the standing figure, as he moved purposefully towards them, but suddenly, another figure appeared at his left, one which Harry had not been paying attention to until it was too late. They collided.

"Oh, I'm so sorry!" the girl exclaimed, "are you ok? I didn't see you".

She was a much older girl, of student age, and clearly one of the service crew, who helped out around the campsite and also acted as instructors for the children as they undertook various activities which the campsite offered. Harry, in that moment, was a little absent-minded towards her, his attentions far more concerned with the vending machine and the figure he had seen standing in front of it. During the short conversation which followed, Harry explained that he had been awoken by the storm during the night, at which she frowned doubtfully at him, commenting that as far as she was aware, there hadn't been any storm.

"Maybe he heard the storm" Harry replied, pointing towards the vending machine and referring to the Scout he had seen standing by it, only to discover that whoever had been there, had now disappeared. She looked in the direction he pointed and then shrugged at him, unsure of who or what he was talking about, and trying to diffuse the awkwardness, she asked Harry which troop he belonged to, and upon hearing his answer, she excitedly told him that she believed that she would be the troop's instructor later in the day for crate stacking, before bidding him farewell. Harry was not very attentive towards her, his mind still focused on the

Scout he had seen, not just the once, but on numerous occasions now, and once he reached the vending machine, whoever it was who had been standing there previously, was nowhere to be seen. After collecting his bottle of fizzy drink, he returned, ponderously, and somewhat confused, back to his site.

The rest of the day was uneventful and Harry, distracted by the activities which the troop undertook seemed to have forgotten about the storm and the other, strange Scouts which he had encountered. The troop did a session of abseiling in the morning, down a very high wall on the side of a climbing tower; this was then followed by an hour of archery, lunch, and then crate stacking in the afternoon – where it was the aim to build a tower of milk crates whilst you climbed, going as high as you could before the tower collapsed. The uneventfulness, however, only lasted until the evening.

The fog had lingered on the site for the entire day, and it made that evening's wide game much more interesting. Spot-light was not a team game, rather an individual one, and the aim was for the Scouts to hide - whether it be amongst the trees, or bushes in the woods, undergrowth, or behind anything else they could find – and try to make their way back in the darkness to base-camp undetected. The leaders were running the game and would be attempting to catch the Scouts in the act of breaking into basecamp, by briefly shining torchlight in various directions at random intervals. As the game started, the Scouts all strode off into the woods to hide, with Harry finding himself an ideal spot amongst some dense and thorny bushes. Naturally, he would have to be careful, but he knew that he would be glad of it as it gave excellent cover, although at some point he would have to move on to a new spot, running the risk of revealing himself. Initially, he was convinced that he was alone and that none of the other Scouts had encroached on his 'safe-zone' as it were, but soon he began to hear whispers, soft and undistinguished at first, before eventually there seemed to be more of a chatter about the place, and it made him wonder if there was indeed a fellow Scout in the vicinity, one who was possibly trying to give him away.

Suddenly, from right next to him, in the darkness, a small voice spoke, as if in an appeal directed at him.

"Please let me play".

Harry jolted, almost falling back amongst the thicket. The voice was one which he didn't recognise, and although he shouldn't have done, he had brought a small torch with him, and as he nervously twitched with a growing panic, he reached into his pocket, drew out his torch, and after a couple of failed attempts, switched it on to see who was there. There was no one there. He shined the torch in as many directions as he could - no longer concerned with the game - but he could find no sign of the owner of the voice which had spoken to him. He switched off the torch, but as soon as he did so, the voice spoke again, this time, from the opposite side to before, as if whoever it was who was speaking were right next to him.

"I like this game.....I would like to play too".

The torch went on again, and again he saw nobody there, but there was rustling in the bush behind him, and as Harry turned, he saw a figure running away through the woods. He got up from his crouching position and gave chase, trying to keep pace. He found it difficult in the dark, with the bushes being rather dense in places, and tree roots providing an extra challenge. He tried to move with some speed, whilst also keeping low, but all the while he felt that whoever he was chasing, was just that much quicker than him. Suddenly, he dropped his torch, and then, predictably he did stumble on something, falling to the ground. There was the sound of laughter - which he presumed to be that of whoever had spoken to him - and it seemed to be close to him to begin with, before drifting away. Shaken, he recovered himself, and on his hands and knees, he made for his torch, which was lying on the ground, beaming light along the surface. But upon reaching his torch, he found something else there, and he realised that it was this which had brought him down.

It was a small wooden block, partially hidden by leaves. It was unremarkable, but for a plaque on the side which Harry noticed upon closer inspection. It read:

IN MEMORY OF FOUR SCOUTS KILLED BY A FALLING TREE
DURING A STORM ON THIS CAMPSITE ON 29TH OCTOBER 1932

As he tried to digest this new piece of information, there was a flash of light and a cry from distance.

"Harry, we can see you".

The leaders' torch shone on him and he was out of the game. As he clambered out of the woods, clearly unsettled, he discovered that he had somehow navigated himself, by accident, round towards another part of the site, despite not coming into contact with any other member of the troop in the process. He was quite sure of this last statement because whoever he had encountered in the woods, if indeed he had encountered anyone at all, had not been one of them. Unusually for him, Harry didn't protest his capture, and when questioned by the leaders on his subduedness, Harry, still trying to make sense of what he had experienced, simply replied that he was fine, he was tired, and was off to bed.

As with the previous night, Harry found himself awake again at around 2am. Although he had managed to get off to sleep without any problems, he found that his sleep was not untroubled, with many strange ideas circling around in his mind. On waking, he felt the urge to relieve himself, and so he got out of his sleeping bag, opened the tent as before and trudged off to the toilet block. It was damp and bitterly cold, and the fog, which seemed to have lingered ever since the previous night, had thickened once more, and with it being so dark as well, Harry quickly abandoned the trip to the toilet block, and decided on using the bushes instead.

On his return to the site, he managed to find his way to the tent - albeit after momentarily losing his bearings in the fog - opened it and got back in, closing the door as if sealing himself inside a tomb, and settled down into the sleeping bag, before closing his eyes. But within moments, he sensed that something was wrong. The tent, due to its age and incessant use, had that musty smell, which, although not necessarily pleasant, was not intolerable; but now the smell was more profound, and had more of a hint of decay about it. It was also bitterly, unnaturally cold inside, and he could now hear rain falling on the roof, whilst the wind was picking up rigorously too.

"Are you scared of the storm?"

He opened his eyes with a start. The sharp shock of the whispered question from out of the darkness hit him hard, and a fear began to grow within him as he realised that it was the same voice as he had heard earlier that evening, during the wide-game, and it had come from inside the tent! He was sure of it. Trembling, he raised himself up, and slowly reached for his torch before turning it on. In the torchlight he could see four other Scouts, all lying, motionless in their sleeping bags, two of them on one side, between him and the door, and another two on the other side of him. One of them must have been the owner of the whispering voice, and, believing it to have been one of the Scouts next to him, who had their back toward him, he leaned over and put his hand on the other's shoulder. They were ice-cold to touch, and they were stiff, as if their flesh had become marble.

With horror, it dawned on Harry that he was most definitely not next to one of his fellow Scouts from his own Patrol, and that whoever it was, there was not a flicker of life within them. He quickly removed his hand, not daring to touch them for a moment longer, and certainly not daring to roll them over to reveal their face. He looked around him and saw that two of the others were also lying with their backs turned toward him and they too appeared to be as still as statues.

The wind outside was clearly now gathering up a ferocity to it; it howled, and the canvas of the tent began to ripple, whilst the wooden poles holding the tent up began to sway and creak. Harry noticed that the 4th Scout was lying on their back, and so he moved closer to them and shone his torch with more precision, soon realising that he didn't recognise them either. It now became clear to him that none of the other occupants inside the tent were Scouts from his own troop, but were those of the strange uniforms, who he had encountered several times since arriving on camp. As he shone the torch, he saw lying there before him, a face he did not recognise, expressionless and fixed in an upwardly position, eyes and mouth shut as if asleep. Their entire body was motionless, their complexion deathly pale, their flesh ice-cold and marble-like, and they were quite clearly not breathing. His torch dropped to the ground and went out. It was clear that apart from Harry, not one of them in that tent was alive! And yet, there came a rustling sound, as if one of them was shifting their body position, and then one of these corpses somehow spoke, directly to him!

"Harry, I'm so scared of the storm!"

As the tent shook violently in the gale, these words proved too much for Harry, who screamed and clambered his way over these hideous beings with sheer and utter panic towards the front of the tent. As he fumbled whilst trying to untie the door, he sensed that there was further movement within the tent, as well as the sound of groanings made by those who were being awakened by disturbances around them. Eventually he managed to untie the door and escape the tent, running away from it as fast as he could through the fog, leaving behind him the sounds of what appeared to be a tree cracking and then crashing to the ground. He moved with speed towards one of the other tents on the site, but before he could reach it, he was grabbed, by one of his leaders who had been woken by his scream.

"What's the matter Harry?" asked the leader, concerned by what he had heard and was now seeing. The night, it should be noted, was still.

Harry was in a state of shock and garbled something to them about the tent and the spectres within it, pointing to where he had just come from through the fog. The leader calmed him, re-assuring him that he had experienced nothing more than a nightmare, but Harry was adamant about what he had seen, continuing to stress that the tent which he had been inside only moments before, contained none of his fellow Scouts from the troop, but 'other' Scouts, who only he had seen since they had arrived, and who were not of the living world. The leader was unsure as to why Harry would claim to have been in a tent at a spot on the site where none of them were camping; of course, when he went to the place indicated, to investigate Harry's claims, it was no surprise to him that he found that there was no tent there, and neither was there any evidence of a tree having recently fallen. He did, however notice one thing which could be of interest, and it was this: the location which Harry indicated, was the spot where had emerged after being caught during the wide game that evening, only yards away from a small wooden block in the ground with a plaque on the side of it.

The rest of the night, although eerily calm and still, saw no storm activity or rain of any kind and the following morning, Harry's mother came to take him home, comforting her trauma-tised son, who never returned to Scouting. The incident proved to be the last straw for the leaders who had grown tired of the con-stant chill and dampness of the fog on site 13. The elderly man-ager was relieved in an 'I told you so', manner when they informed him of their desire to relocate, and it was arranged for the troop to move that very morning to a different site. After changing sites, the troop experienced no further trouble for the rest of the week, whilst it was decided that site 13 would be off-limits to all, with no exceptions.

The epilogue to the story must belong to the manager himself, who had this to say of Harry's encounters when quizzed by the leaders:

"Can't say I'm surprised, to be honest with you. That site has been a strange one ever since the storm of '32. Those poor boys... crushed they was...sleeping in their tent when the tree come down on top of it...never stood a chance. I try not to go there my-self...reckon I saw them there once, lingering in the bushes, sort of watching me they was...and I ain't been the only one who seen 'em neither...don't think their souls ever left the place...s'pose that's why there's a funny atmosphere about the place, with the fog and all that. Sometimes, I think, if they take a likin' to you, you might see 'em in other places too...like they want you to be their friends or summat. I did try and warn you…...."

"You said that one of the boys survived?" cut in one of the leaders, inquisitively.

"Went out to go to toilet, didn't he" was the reply. "Only gone a few moments and it just came down and he missed it. Call it luck if you want, but I don't reckon it was luck to see what he saw, poor kid. Don't know what happened to 'im after that. Mind you, your young lad might have seen everything if he had been in that tent any longer that he was….gawd knows what would have happened….it could've been five of 'em gone!"

The Painted Box

"So, you've come about the box, then?" the bespectacled man called out, as I walked across the green. I wasn't sure what business it was of his, but as I passed, he seemed to have a keen interest in my arrival. "If my old mum were still alive, she would tell you to stay away from it or burn it" he continued.

The small town I had come to borders onto the Kent Weald and sits just outside the M25, along the main 'A' road running parallel to the motorway. Despite the significant volume of traffic which passes through, it has in comparison to towns of similar size further into London, a sleepy quality to it. The main feature of the town is a pretty green surrounded by little shops and cafés, with the grass sloping upwards towards the 14th century church, with its bell tower topped by a spire shaped like a witch's hat. Also present on the green are statues of two famous Britons, both of whom were significant local residents (both of their residencies are open to the public, courtesy of the National Trust). I must say that, as you walk around the town, you do get the impression that apart from the addition of the main road, little has changed there since

Georgian times.

The box in question had been discovered in the local Scout hut by some of the older Scouts in the troop, during a weekend clear-out of one of the storerooms, which had become a damp infested junk-space. It was found sitting there in the corner of the room, hidden away under some elderly tents and other items past their best condition, and it clearly hadn't been exposed to the light of day for many years. It was wooden, with rope for handles on either side, was large enough to contain several reams of A4 paper and was painted half in yellow and half in black, which was the colour scheme associated with the Wolves patrol. Once the Scouts who found it had blown the cobwebs and dust away, they slowly opened the lid and found that inside, it contained old Scouting papers pertaining to the troop and the Wolves patrol, dating from the time when the box had last been in use.

When I reached the Scout hut - a small, slightly shabby looking building - I was greeted by the main leader, a balding man named Grayson, who had contacted me via my website, regarding strange things which had been occurring ever since the box's discovery. On first examining the box, I found it to be just that...a box. It seemed innocuous enough, a simple, inanimate wooden painted box, more a relic of a bygone age than anything else; an object that had likely had many years of usage before being forgotten about and abandoned, to eventually succumb to rot or the infestation of woodlouse. Grayson told me that he had once been a Scout there too, and remembered there being other boxes like this, one for each of the Patrols, made by someone who had been new to the area. This box's discovery had come as something of a surprise to Grayson, as he had believed that all of them had been destroyed over the years, for various reasons, although there had obviously been some kind of oversight with regards to this one. Quite why it had survived the cull and had been hidden away in the manner that it had, was a mystery to him. When reflecting upon it, he said that he felt there was something unusual about the box, although he found it difficult to elaborate any further, only adding that he wondered whether it was not meant to have been found, and that maybe, it should have remained hidden.

In the tone of an aside, Grayson informed me that some of the children at the Scout Troop had become concerned that there was a stray animal prowling around the grounds. They had heard it moving in the bushes and banks of nettles, breathing heavily, and apparently, one of them had caught a glimpse of its eyes. It should be noted, however, that the Scout in question was not entirely sure that it had been eyes which they had seen. The reason for this doubt came from the fact that what they saw, were two small red circles glaring at them; and as eyes were not usually of such a striking colour as the bright red dots on display, the idea of them being eyes was surely a ridiculous one.

I found myself obliged to survey the grounds outside the Scout hut, on Grayson's insistence, just in case the supposed sightings introduced a new element to proceedings. I found that around the back of the building, the nettles were so dense that it seemed that either there was some kind of infestation or that the area had been poorly maintained and neglected for several years, and judging by the building itself, I preferred the latter explanation. It was very much like a jungle there, as if the Triffids had taken over the grounds, but despite this, I can confirm that I found no animal lurking there, although I did come across some signs in the grass that it may have been trodden on by something, but this being the countryside, I felt that this would not be unusual or cause great alarm.

As I walked back towards the green and the town centre, my mind was distracted by thoughts of the box, and the mystery surrounding the apparent sightings of the creature around the Scout hut grounds. I passed a small cottage by the side of the road, and as I did so, I was startled by a loud thud, as something threw itself violently at the front gate, beyond which a small stone path led through a pretty garden. It was a dog - I didn't see which breed - and it barked loudly and vigorously at me, as if warning me to keep away at all costs. I moved on as quickly as I could, but as I continued, it seemed as though every dog I encountered viewed me with a deep suspicion, as if I were some kind of enemy and a threat to them. They seemed to become very defensive and growled menacingly at me, and I began to feel rather uneasy and also rather unwelcome.

Deeply distracted by the unsettling tone, which was beginning to develop, I didn't pay attention to where I was going and nearly walked straight into an oncoming elderly lady. She too had a dog, a massive, light brown Great Dane, which growled in my direction, even more threateningly than the others had.

"Sampson! Stop it at once!" she shouted. I apologised to her. "He's normally so good around people" she replied, "even strangers. I don't know what has gotten into him, there has never been any problems with him before; in fact, all of the dogs around here are usually so gentle and well trained, well, that was...until the other Saturday...oh there was a terrible howling that night, Sampson was at it for hours, and he wasn't the only one neither! Hasn't been himself since"

Another voice suddenly interjected from behind me, one that I recognised.

"They found that box the other Saturday, didn't they" he stated. It was the man who had called out to me earlier that morning. He introduced himself as the churchwarden and said that he too had heard the howling that night and that it was such a terrible din, it seemed that every dog in the town was in full voice, howling in unison. The lady tentatively agreed with him, and as they talked for a few moments, I wondered quite what connection the man was making between the howling dogs and the seemingly innocuous discovery of the box, why it was of concern to him, and how fast news circulated around the area.

After a brief discussion, the lady moved on, pulling desperately at Sampson as she went - in an attempt keep him under control - as he still seemed to be perturbed by something, and it did concern me that that 'something' was related to my presence there.

The churchwarden looked at me through his glasses. He was in his 60s and had the air of someone who had lived in the town all his life. From the way he spoke, I had the impression that he knew something about what had been going on but was being very coy about it. He took me up to the church, as he wanted to show me something, and once inside, we headed to the vestry, walking over to a small cabinet, which he began to move away from the wall. By moving the cabinet, he revealed a small wooden panel, which had been hidden from view. The panel showed a scene painted onto it featuring three men, and to their right, a fearful skeleton draped in a long black shawl and grinning at them with evil intent. It reminded me of one of those doom paintings created in the Middle Ages - which are often found in ancient parish churches and portray the Last Judgement - not least because of the style, but also because of the grimness of it and the feeling of damnation which emanated from it when viewed. It certainly sent a little shiver down my back, as if the skeletal figure itself had run its finger along my spine.

"No one has seen this for around 50 years" he said, warning me quite firmly not to touch it. I did wonder if it being hidden away had contributed to its remarkably good condition. "It's Medieval" he continued "and depicts three sinners and the Reaper, and was made locally".

I wondered why I was being shown this, and he told me that it had been hidden away after one of his predecessors had been driven mad by it, claiming that he had encountered 'King Death' himself, rising up from out of the grounds outside the church one evening, as if making an appearance - exactly as it was seen in the picture - to pass judgement on the living. The use of the name 'King Death' was curious and rather telling. It suggested to me that even now, there was still deep superstition and acceptance of the supernatural entrenched in the minds of some within the community, and further indication of this followed.

"My old mum used to say" he added, "that if anyone had any sense, they wouldn't make things using materials from around here...bad wood, you see".

I asked him what he meant by that, and his answer was

sadly rather vague, but from what I gathered, there was some local superstition surrounding the trees in the nearby woods. Apparently, the trees had been imbued with 'unnatural properties' centuries or millennia ago; although quite what was meant by 'unnatural properties', I couldn't really tell, as the man was not as forthcoming with information as I would have liked, but I surmised that the inference was that some sort of sorcery or witchcraft was involved.

I must say that I got the impression that despite his position in the Church, the man was very much immersed in the local superstitions. He seemed to be suggesting, as ridiculous as it sounds, that he was of the opinion that the retched figure in the painting I had been shown, had manifested itself into real life - revealing itself to his predecessor in the churchyard - by way of its being painted onto wood taken from these trees!

Upon leaving the church, I made a brief inspection of the grounds, and as you would expect, I could find nothing which indicated anything untoward, although I must confess that I wasn't certain of what to look for, when searching for the presence, at any time, of the manifestation of the figure of Death. By now, it had become apparent that the day had advanced further along than previously thought, and was dangerously bordering on the surreal. Several different strands of interest had emerged, their connection and relevance unclear, and I felt that it was now time to head for home, to try to untangle my thoughts, and to rest.

Overnight, I had, I must declare to you, a troubled sleep. As I dreamt, a soundtrack of constant howling, made it seemed, by dogs in their dozens - or maybe even hundreds – played in the background. In one particular dream, I found myself walking along a street I knew well, it being local to me. It was very early in the morning, prior to dawn and the collection of rubbish, and as I walked along, I saw black sacks stacked together and left on the pavement outside of buildings, in readiness to be taken away. One of these collections of sacks caught my eye as I approached and suddenly, a feeling of dread came upon me. I stopped abruptly, around 10m away, and watched with some amazement as the sacks seemed to begin rustling. As I stared, not only did the sacks rustle, but they also started to move, in a somewhat awkward fashion, as one might expect to see of some creature waking from its slumber. And then, the shape – and I could see that it was no longer a collection of black rubbish sacks – rose slowly into a standing position, to become a figure in black, which I reckoned to be malevolent. I knew what the figure was, and had it not been obscured by the darkness of pre-dawn, I would have been familiar with the awful grin that it had on its face, as I had seen it in the picture in the church.

My initial curiosity for the scene had by now disappeared totally, and in its place, fear of what was unfolding before me had not only grown, but now threatened to overwhelm me, and somehow, I forced myself awake. It had been a horrible image, of course it had, and yet, I felt that I was only observing it, and that its attention was not necessarily directed at me, but another person. Although the location was relevant to me, it was as if the vision had actually been someone else's, namely, I realised, that of the former churchwarden, who I had been made aware of only hours before. Was this, I pondered, a warning? If 'King Death', as he had been named, had been the entity of horror that had confronted the former churchwarden, was there another, greater entity of horror - one that was as yet unknown - for me to face?

The following morning, I took the bus back to the town and made my way straight to the Scout hut, where I was given access and allowed to have a look around. Inside, the painted box was there, sitting on a table at the back. It was flanked by the Union flag on a small wooden pole on one side, and a large painted version of the Scout badge (a fleur-de-lis surrounded by a ring of rope, with a purple background) painted on the wall behind it on the other. What struck me was how - and I hadn't really this noticed before - it seemed to sit there, almost arrogantly - all powerful - as if it were some kind of shrine or altar, and I felt compelled to touch it. Of course, I had examined it thoroughly the previous day, but this time, it felt different, as if something seemed to be urging me forwards, calling me to lay my hand on it, like I would a holy relic. I did touch it but surprisingly, disappointingly, and despite the compulsion I had felt, touching the box brought no 'experience', religious, supernatural, or otherwise. It just seemed to sit there, as if waiting for something.

I decided to go for a hike through the woods to clear my mind and attempt to make some sense of the developments thus far, unclear as to what the central problem actually was, or how the numerous strands interwove with each other. Additionally, I felt that after hearing the thoughts of the churchwarden, the woods also required investigation.

The trees were a wonderful golden colour for autumn, the sun was bright, and the temperature was mild. I walked for hours, and heard birds squawking in the distance, the breeze filtering through the trees, and my boots crunching through the leaves on the ground. At times, my mind wandered, overflowing with theories and hypotheses about what may have been going on, and what forces may or may not have been at work throughout the affair so far. I half expected to find, as I walked, evidence of some local Pagan customs, such as objects with mysterious messages or meanings hanging from the trees, but came across nothing. In some ways, the lack of anything made me slightly more uneasy for some reason, as did the lack of any signs of human activity.

As I approached a clearing, late in the afternoon, I came across an ornate but weathered and rusting set of table and chairs which, while they wouldn't have looked out of place in a nice Victorian garden on a warm sunny day with tea and scones having been served, most certainly did here. I decided to rest, and as I sat there, I heard something new, something menacing. My ears pricked up, and I decided that it was the sound of something treading on the leaves, treading carefully, as if it was watching, stalking, hunting.

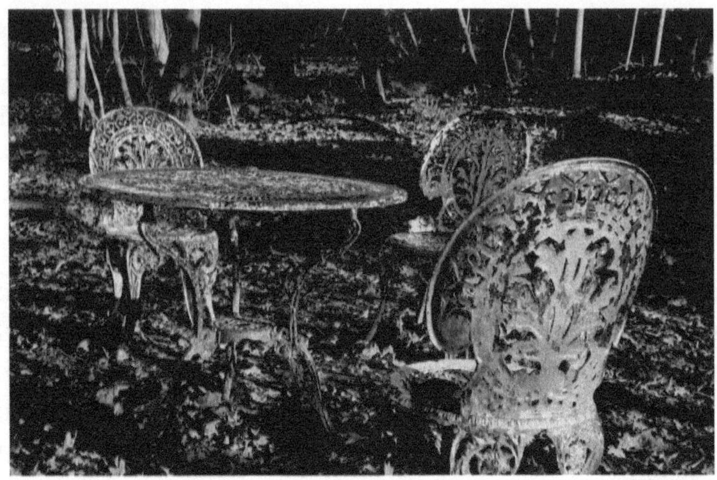

Then, I heard a great howl pierce through the autumn air and it sent a shockwave right through me. It wasn't the sound of a dog barking excitedly as it explored the woods on an afternoon walk with its owner...but the sound of something else: it was certainly canine, but not, I thought, a sound made by an Earthly, natural being. Whatever creature had made this horrible sound, I knew that it had a menacing intent. I stood up in an instant and spun round, searching in all directions, hoping, praying that I wouldn't see the source of the great howl I had heard, but then, I stopped spinning, as I saw, in the bushes behind me, two piercing red eyes, clearly fixed upon me. Stunned, I began to shake with terror. I knew that these were the red eyes which had been spotted in the Scout hut grounds, and that I had previously dismissed them; but here they now were, and they appeared to be very real and staring at me with malice. Slowly, gingerly, I began to walk away. As I did so, the creature slowly emerged from the bushes, and I caught a glimpse first of its teeth – which appeared razor sharp and ready to tear into flesh - and then its claws. I backed further away, moving quickly as I did so and then turned before I could see any more of it and broke into a run. The creature howled horribly once again, as if exciting itself about the chase, and then followed in pursuit picking up pace and stomping on the ground as it went. I dared not look back as I ran, but I had no need to do so when confirming that a race for my survival was indeed afoot, as I heard it behind me, growling menacingly, readying itself to pounce at the first opportunity of any weakness in myself.

The light was now fading fast, and I decided to veer from the track I was on, trying desperately to lose it, but as I kept running, dusk seemed to come with a shocking rapidity. I knew that as it got ever darker, the danger to my very existence heightened, as although I would find it increasingly impossible to navigate, the creature would likely have no difficulty in tracking me down in the dark. Suddenly, I came to a stop, looked around, and saw that the trees all looked exactly the same and I realised that I had lost my way! Then, for a moment, it seemed that, maybe, I had shaken the creature off my scent, and I began to hope that salvation would come to me after all, but devastatingly, I heard it growl once more, louder and closer than before. Clearly, I had not been able to lose it, and I began to wonder, with a sinking feeling, if I ever could.

It was now totally dark, save for the light from the moon, and I ran again, in desperation, hoping to find my way, but I knew that the creature was now gaining on me, and preparing to strike. My lungs began to hurt and I was in a state of panic. I knew that not only could I not outrun it, but I also couldn't see where I was going, and that on all counts it had a crushing advantage over me. Eventually, I seemed to emerge into a clearing, and here, I realised that my body had nothing left in the tank and finally I admitted defeat, a defeat that I was sure would be a final, fatal one. I forced myself to a standstill and began to turn, readying myself to face the creature that would bring about my end. As I turned, I saw it charge out of the trees, its red eyes filled with hate. I closed my own eyes as tears flowed and my body shook with terror.

BANG!

There was a gunshot and I fell to the ground. The creature let out an awful noise and fled, scared off by the shot. I opened my eyes and looked up, and in the moonlight, I saw a figure standing in the middle of the clearing, holding a rifle.

"Are you ok?" he shouted as he came over to me - his head-torch now glowing - helping me to my feet. When I looked back into his face, I discovered that it had been the churchwarden who had saved me.

"Did you kill it?" I asked, breathlessly, trying to regain a measure of control over my senses and emotions.

"No, wounded maybe, but it was just a warning shot" he replied, "my old mum told me that there is only one way to deal with 'King Wolf', and she were always right". I noted the similarity between his naming of the creature, and the way he had spoken of the Grim Reaper the previous day. I was, of course, shaken and rather bemused by everything, but also exceedingly grateful for his timely intervention and for saving my life. In that moment he seemed to have changed from coming across as a scratchy, narrow-minded, and superstitious local simpleton, into someone who had authority, confidence, and a sense of doing what was right and necessary.

"Come" he said, offering his hand in support "it is time we put an end to this".

That evening, with Grayson's permission, we burnt the painted box on a bonfire in the Scout hut grounds. As it burnt, the wood let off a strange, hideous, unnatural odour, unlike anything I had smelt before. All the while, I noticed a horrible howling of dogs that filled the night air, as if they were in mourning.

"See, what did I tell you…bad wood" the churchwarden commented, before informing me that it was common knowledge around the locality that the wood from the trees was 'bad'. Only 'outsiders', as he called them, ever really ventured out into the woods for walks as locals knew to stay away, and only 'newcomers' who knew no differently, would use wood from those trees as materials, for things such as the Church painting or the wooden Scout boxes, for example. With this, it at last became clear to me how all the various strands - which had not seemed particularly compatible with each other at first - came together.

As we talked, he described to me the creature which he had seen coming up behind me from the woods. Of course, it had been very dark, despite the moonlight, so it was perhaps difficult to see clearly, but he said that he thought it the largest and most terrifying wolf he had known. It had, he said, piercing red eyes filled with hate, hair horribly matted, mouth foaming with saliva, and teeth so sharp that they would have ripped a person to shreds with very little effort. Also, he said, it was as if the Devil himself had been its creator.

The churchwarden confirmed that he knew of the boxes, courtesy of his predecessor, and that after hearing of the discovery of this final box – which had come as a surprise to him as he had not been aware that any of the boxes had survived – had become gravely concerned at what would ensue as a result, hence his warnings to stay away from it. He informed us that as the church was a listed building, he had been unable to have the painting of the three men and 'King Death' removed and destroyed, despite his belief that it would be the correct thing to do. Instead, he declared that 'extra steps' would be taken to ensure that it wouldn't be seen by anyone ever again. I guessed that he had only shown it to me thinking that I would understand and accept the superstitions he told of, make the connection between the painting and the box, and then take the appropriate action.

After the box had been completely burnt, the howling stopped and there appeared to be a return to normality and solitude amongst the local canine community. I can tell you that I had no more nightly visions like those I described to you, probably because I had, thanks to the intervention of the churchwarden, escaped the wrath of 'King Wolf' itself, the thing that had been my horror to face. There were no more sightings of any creature in the grounds of the Scout hut either, nor were there any other strange occurrences, and as far as I know, this proved to be the end of the matter.

Ring a Ring O'Roses

About a week ago, the local Scout Group's time capsule was opened, at the expressed wish of those who had set it down when the construction of the Group's headquarters was begun over 60 years ago. It had been buried beneath the foundations, towards the rear of the building and directly underneath the Group's Union flag which they used for ceremonies during their weekly meetings, the location marked by a small concrete slab inscribed with the words:

THIS CAPSULE WAS PLACED HERE AMONG THE
FOUNDATIONS OF ------- HALL
BY MRS ETHEL JOHNSON, AKELA
TO BE OPENED ON --JULY 2015

The small metal box was painted black and locked using padlocked clasps either side of a central lock, the keys to which were in the possession of the Group Scout Leader, having been passed down to them by their predecessors. Inside was the usual collection of trinkets showing life as a Scout in the 1950's such as homemade woggles, badges, garters, photographs and letters, many of which had kept to a surprisingly good condition. Also included were some rather curious pieces of creative writing, clearly demonstrating the imaginations of children of the 1950s with regards to how they saw the future, and what they thought life would be like in the 21st century.

I had been invited to attend the ceremony at which the box was recovered and opened, and I can tell you that it was a wonderful day. Thankfully, the weather was kind, and it meant that there could be celebrations outside; so, a barbeque was the order of the day, and plenty of wonderful food and drink was had by those in attendance, with there also being games and other entertainments for the children. For myself, it was something of a reunion, as I had been a former Scout at the Group, and it was good to catch-up with some of those who I hadn't seen in many years. It was certainly fascinating to see how some of them had gotten on in adult life: I discovered that one of them was now married and had three children, along with a job in finance in the City; another had recently returned from a 6 month sojourn in Australia, and was telling of their adventures; while one of the others was currently coaching youngsters at the local cricket club. I, being a writer with an interest in history, had seen the event not only as an opportunity to meet up again with former comrades, but also to gain material for a project I had been contemplating for some time, namely researching the history of Scouting in the local area.

I had requested to be granted special access to whatever was found in the box, with the purpose of using the items as material for my project, and my request was granted. Of course, all the usual items which I have already described to you were of great interest, but also among the items inside the capsule, was a bound leather journal - size A5 - belonging to one Edgar Athelstan. It was an inclusion which at first seemed rather baffling, as there was no record of him being a member of the Group. In fact, after doing some research, I discovered that he was an archaeologist and teacher at University College, and, intrigued, I decided that I would make it a new priority of mine to read the journal, to find out why an archaeologist's journal had found its way into a Scout Group's time capsule. What I found was extraordinary and below I give a summary of the relevant parts:

***

12th May 1955

We received a very interesting letter today from George Thurlow, a landscaper and architect who is currently laying foundations for a Scout Hut in -------- in Kent. According to his letter, some human remains have been found at the site, which is rather exciting, and he has requested that someone from the university could attend and oversee an investigation.

From what I understand, he has requested that we act with some haste, and having confirmed the university's interest, it has been agreed that I shall head down to -------- for an initial survey of the site, before reporting my findings ahead of further investigation.

I suspect I shall be going down some time early next week, as it seems they don't want there to be too long a delay to the building work.

18th May 1955

I went down to -------- today, picking up the 10:21 train from Charing Cross. These new electric trains are very comfortable and nowhere near as noisy or smoky as the old steam trains, but they just don't have the same magic. That said, with it being a hot day, I was able to have the window open next to where I sat, and without the smoke and soot that accompanies steam trains, it was most pleasant as I was able to breath in fresh air and allow myself to peek my head out of the window every now and then, albeit briefly, to have a better of view of the journey. The only inconvenience is that by sitting right by the doors, at every station, one's personal space is invaded as someone inevitably opens the door right by where you are and climbs over you to either join or disembark. The journey itself is an interesting one; not terribly scenic, but heavily industrial, and fascinating from the point of view of seeing how London has expanded along the Thames and has become a vastly different city to that of say, 300 years ago.

Anyway, what an extraordinary day it's been. When I arrived, I was greeted by Mr Thurlow himself: a big, burly fellow in his sixties, balding and sweating profusely - due mainly to the weather, but also, I suspected, as a result of poor health brought on by being overweight. He was wearing a brown woollen suit, which seemed rather inappropriate for the conditions of the day, and on greeting me, he removed his trilby hat and shook my hand, rather moistly. After exchanging initial pleasantries, he escorted me to his motor car, which took us on the journey up the hill from the station and to the main part of the town. As we went, he told me some of the history of the area, including a tale about the area around the station being flooded by the great tidal surge of '53

On reaching the site, which was on the corner of a bend in a lane just off the main high-street, I also met Mrs Ethel Johnson, the Akela and leader of the Group - a strong, no-nonsense sort of a woman, with a secretarial look to her, with her grey perm and glasses, and a prim and proper complexion - who I think I shall get along with just grand! The pair of them took me on a tour of the site; it's a fielded area which backs on to a local school, with the spire of the parish church seen to the left of it, as well as the back of a builder's yard, further along up the lane.

I was shown the spot where the bodies were found - five of them so far – and what struck me was that they looked as though they had just been thrown into the graves (if I can even call them graves) as seen by the way the bodies were positioned. My initial theory is that we may be dealing here with a group burial, and naturally, we are going to need to set up a proper dig here to investigate what has been discovered, what more there is to find, and what can be revealed about the site and what went on here.

22nd May 1955

The area where the Scout hut is going to be built has been turned into a big archaeological dig with over a dozen volunteers and members of the University team scratching away at the soil with trowels and brushes, desperately trying to uncover the secrets of what occurred here. I have also been getting my hands dirty, as it were, as I do find it invigorating to roll up my sleeves and be on my knees in the dirt -

frustratingly laborious as it may be sometimes - as the excitement and anticipation of uncovering something does thrill the soul of someone such as myself, who has a fascination for the past.

We've found around 20 bodies up to now, which I think is rather a lot for an unmarked burial ground, and I now believe that we are dealing with a mass burial of some kind. I want to try that new carbon-dating method to date some of these bodies, and I have made enquiries with my colleagues in other departments at the university, asking whether we can use their equipment, to provide us with more details as to when these bodies may be from. I do hope that we shan't discover that they are recent, as that may be rather awkward and require the intervention of local authorities such as the police, who would almost certainly view the site as a crime scene, and besides, it would be far more exciting, from an archaeological point of view, to find that we have uncovered bodies from hundreds of years ago!

24th May 1955

I found a body myself today, and it appears to have been slightly set apart from the rest. At first, I uncovered what appeared to be two glass circles, each surrounded by metallic rings, the glass of each broken. They were found with fragments of what appeared to be leather, and I did wonder if they were part a hood of some kind, which hadn't survived. I put the two glass circles up to my own eyes, and although I could not see through them, I could certainly imagine them being used as eye-pieces. As I investigated further, it became apparent that a body was with them, a large one at that, seemingly rather tall and no doubt intimidating when alive, and I saw that in one hand, it appeared to have been holding some sort of metal instrument. Ideas quickly came to me as to who this might have been...a doctor perhaps? A blacksmith?

It's strange because although I was excited by the discovery, I began to feel slightly uneasy. As I uncovered the body, I noticed that there was a change in the temperature; it has been another very warm day, and yet a sharp chill developed in the air as the breeze picked up, almost without signalling a warning, and I felt the hairs on the back of my neck stand on end, as if something at the back of my mind was telling me that not everything in that moment was as it should be, whereas before it had been.

27th May 1955

The body I found the other day appears to have been the last one, and in some ways, it seems as though it is rather significant that it was indeed the last that was found and was also separate from the others. The bodies have been extracted from the site and transported to London, and I am now back at the University doing some tests to see if we can find out when they are from, and hopefully we shan't have to wait too long for the results.

I am certainly very curious about the whole affair, and also a little regretful, as if I would rather not have been the one who had volunteered to get involved. You see, I haven't been able to shake off this feeling of unease that has been growing over the last few days, and I keep looking over my shoulder as if someone is there, watching me. Of course, there isn't anyone there; well, there are my fellow colleagues, but that is not what I mean – I don't really know how to describe it at present – no, I mean someone, or something else.

1st June 1955

I fear that I'm becoming paranoid. It seems to me that someone is following me, wherever I am going, and I do not like it at all. It took me 2 hours to get to the University yesterday as I double-backed on myself several times in attempting to lose them, but to no avail, and in the end, I decided to try as best I could to ignore them and pretend that it was just my imagination going into overdrive, and that work would alleviate my anxiety and I would come to realise that I am acting ridiculously. And yet, it didn't work, as I was followed on my way home too. The thing is, I haven't actually seen anyone following me yet, and in fact it is more of a 'feeling' that I have. Indeed, whenever I turn around to catch a sight of my possible follower, I see no-one there.

2nd June 1955

This morning, I finally caught some sort of glimpse of my stalker (I'm going to call them that now, as that is what I believe them to be). As I said, it was only a glimpse of them, and more in the corner of my eye rather than a full-on view of them. It was just after exiting the Underground Station at Russell Square, and they seemed to emerge from a small crowd dispersing behind me. From what I could discern from my peripheral vision, I believe that they were quite tall, and appeared to be wearing a long dark cloak and a wide brimmed hat. Unfortunately, that was the extent of my view, as once again, upon turning around fully, it appeared that there was no one of any distinction there, with the only people being the average commuters.

I am becoming rather concerned, and am contemplating, reporting it to the police, but surely before I do that, I would need to have more tangible proof that someone is indeed stalking me, and for that I need to actually see them with unobscured vision.

7th June 1955

I am still waiting for the carbon-dating results. I have spoken with others who were present at the dig and enquired of them if they have been having any unusual experiences. So far, it seems that I am the only one who has encountered anything untoward. I could tell you more of my feelings of being followed, but fear that although they are indeed concerning, something else has overtaken them and will prove to be far more alarming:

I'm having nightmares. They began two nights ago and seem to be recurring. In them, my vision is blurred and my breathing heavy and muffled, as if I am wearing something over my head, such as a hood of some description, with my eyes peering through pieces of glass. I appear to be walking down a small, filthy alleyway, with wooden buildings on either side, stacking up several levels, to the point whereby they block out a significant amount of sunlight. I can see people lying in the streets, helpless, motionless; some quite clearly dead, others barely alive and in agony - their flesh dirty and rotting, with tiny, biting creatures crawling all over - as they wait endlessly for their final moments on Earth. Although I cannot smell it, I am aware of the foulest of stenches, and in the background a church bell tolls hauntingly, overriding the cries of agony from all around me. I never seem to make it to the end of the alleyway as I dream, the horror of what I am seeing being too much for me to endure, and yet, I know that somehow what

I see is of importance, and that I will find myself there once again. I also feel that although rather vivid, what I am witnessing seems to be through another's eyes rather than my own.

17th June 1955

I must seek help as I can't sleep properly and I'm losing weight due to a lack of appetite. My nightmares are becoming more vivid, more terrifying with each occurrence, and I am now trying to keep myself awake, in the hope of avoiding slipping into whatever foul and depraved world I have been finding myself in my sleep.

Even when I daydream, I find that I am unable to escape the hellish visions! Let me give you an example: I was in my living room yesterday evening, sitting in my favourite comfortable chair, listening to the radio with my feet curled up and my blanket around me. I was feeling rather cosy, and after a long and tiring day, a little drowsy too, and for a few moments, as I began drifting towards sleep, I perceived that an extraordinary change occurred, because instead of my blanket, it seemed that I was now being surrounded by a great number of black rats, all sniffing and scratching about me, emitting an awful noise of high-pitched squeaking! It startled me enormously, and I yelped with alarm, waking fully and with some vigour, and although I found that it was indeed my blanket, and not those hideous rodents which accompanied me, my skin felt dirty, and itching all over, to such an extent that I felt it necessary to run myself a bath as quickly as possible!

I must seek help.

19th June 1955

I feel as if only my work is keeping me sane at present. The carbon-dating results were announced this morning and they suggest that the bodies are from the 1600s, which tallies with some suspicions I have been musing to myself over recent days.

Following on from the results, I decided to undertake some further research this afternoon and discovered some old parish records for the area which suggest that this land was used as a plague pit during an outbreak in 1665. At the time there was a small settlement and pest house here, around 17 miles from the Centre of London. The outbreak here ran concurrently with the one which hit the Capital and it seems that it took off rather quickly, which would account for the mass burial - made in such haste that it hadn't been taken into account that the ground was unconsecrated. Has any of this got anything to do with my nightmares? I certainly feel that it is important that we run tests on the bodies to see if there are any traces of the plague bacteria, Yersinia Pestis on them.

22nd June 1955

I returned to -------- today to inform Mr Thurlow and Mrs Johnson of our findings, and recommend to them that in my opinion, construction should be postponed until further examination of the site was conducted. I also suggested – although this was more for my own piece of mind rather than anything else - that they may wish to contact the local vicar and have the ground of the site consecrated. Of course, I didn't say anything to them of my own experiences, as I would have come across rather foolishly; after all, who would believe me? Surely, what I have already put down in this journal would be nonsense.....and yet they have happened to me, and although I can not necessarily provide proof, my own eye-witness accounts are not the work of an over-imaginative mind trying to create some sort of fiction.

I am still being followed. As I spent a diversionary hour this afternoon exploring the local area, I walked past a nearby primary school and the children in the playground were playing, dancing and singing. It was a large area, tarmacked and surrounded by a brick wall about 2ft high, with tall black metal railings atop. As I walked past, I recognised the song they were singing, and imagine my surprise, and indeed my shock, when I realised that they sang 'Ring a Ring O'Roses'. I stopped, and peered at them, and suddenly they too stopped what they were doing, all of them at once, as if part of some kind of collective, and stared back at me. It was dreadfully creepy, and softly, quietly, one or two of them began to sing again, the same song as before, whilst continuing to stare at me! Then I realised, that they weren't necessarily staring at me, but behind me, at someone, or something, their eyes fixed upon it. I trembled with a growing terror, sweat appearing on my brow, and slowly I turned around to see what was behind me, to see what they were staring at. As I did so, from out of the corner of my eye I saw the shape of a figure standing several feet away from me - I knew it instantly to be the figure which had been stalking me – and with every tiny movement I made as I rotated, it seemed to creep bit by bit into my fuller vision. All the while I could hear the school children's song echoing hauntingly around me:

Ring a Ring O'Roses,
A pocket full of posies,
A-tishoo! A-tishoo!
We all fall down!

As the last line of the verse rang out and the figure finally began to emerge fully into my vision, I felt my consciousness drain away from me, before everything blurred and then turned to complete darkness. It was the final thing I can remember from the episode, and the next thing I know, I found myself waking on a bed in the local doctor's surgery, with Mrs Johnson standing beside me. Apparently, I fainted, most likely, the doctor said, due to dehydration whilst walking past the school, and had been spotted in the act of falling by some of the children. They alerted their teacher, who then came to my aid, before calling for the doctor.

I was sent home - the university was, of course, informed of the developments - and told to rest, hence why I find myself writing in my journal whilst sitting at home at 3 o'clock in the afternoon. Maybe, I will now endeavour to seek the help that I perhaps need, but who would listen to me? Is it that my only way of communicating my troubles is through this journal, as whoever will read this will be more inclined to listen to my experiences and be non-judgmental and non-dismissive?

I was still not able to get a proper glimpse of who, or what seems to be stalking me, having blacked-out before it revealed itself fully to me. I wonder, too, if it is connected to my dreams and what all of this means in the grand scheme of what is currently happening.

27th June 1955
I must seek help!

Last night my nightmare was the most terrible of all. This time, I seemed to waken, lying in my bed, all hot and sweaty, as if I had been overcome by some horrid fever. Whilst I felt weaker than usual, I did have some strength, and after reaching for and then sipping from a glass of water from my bedside, I made my way to my bathroom and turned on the small light once there. It was as I approached the sink - above which rests a large mirror – in order to wash with cold water, that I first felt something under my armpit. A concern came over me in that moment and I decided to examine myself in the mirror, so I undid my pyjama shirt buttons, and with some trepidation I reached towards my armpit, worried as to what I may find. What I felt with my fingers, chilled me in an instant, and fear began to grip me as I had a vague inclination of the horror yet to come. I decided to take off my pyjama shirt with speed, and looking into the mirror, almost with reluctance, as if I could not bring myself to confirm what I already suspected, I raised my arm.

And there it was: the large, pussy, revolting, black and blue buboe which I had felt only moments before. It was the size of an apricot and it bulged hideously out of my armpit; and it wasn't just the one armpit which was affected either, because as I quickly discovered, it was both of them. And then, to my further horror, I noticed another of these things, having seemingly sprung up from nowhere, gruesomely placed on the side of my neck...and all of this told me that I was infected with the plague! The shock of it all overwhelmed me, as surely, I tried telling myself - due to the fever which I appeared to have - I had become delirious, and it was all just an hallucination aided by the dimness of the light. But however much I attempted to convince myself that none of this was actually happening, I saw too, above me on the glass of the mirror in red paint, a cross and the words "Lord have mercy upon us!"

Then, emerging out of the darkness from behind me, came THE figure, the being which had been stalking me since I had disturbed its resting place over a month ago. I noticed that in its hand was a medical instrument. I turned around to finally face it and, unable to avert my eyes, I saw staring directly back at me the brown leather hood with the long crow's beak and two broken glass eyes of...the plague doctor!

I screamed and in the next moment I was back at the site of the dig, only now I wasn't standing there as an archaeologist examining an extraordinary find, but as a poor lifeless wretch lying on a cart. Then I felt myself roll as the cart was tipped and I fell downwards, to find myself lying, face upwards inside a pit, THE pit, the one which had been discovered and had brought me to --------- in the first place. I was surrounded by dozens of other lifeless bodies, all of them pale, blistered, rotting, and emitting a terrible stench. Looking down at me from above was the plague doctor himself, and as a bell tolled ominously in the background, he walked away as other figures approached, holding spades, and began to throw dirt in my direction. I knew then that I was to be buried, and even though I knew they would not hear me, I screamed as loudly and as mightily as I could.

I awoke, at first deeply distressed at what I had experienced (and this time it had quite clearly been through my own eyes, and not anybody else's), but subsequently relieved that, upon examining myself, I appeared healthy and free of plague, thank the Lord!

11th July 1955

The nightmares have ceased, and I no longer feel that I am being followed. It seems as if a huge weight has been taken off my shoulders, as two days ago the bodies of all those found were buried in the local Church grounds. The speed of it surprised me, and from a professional point of view it feels rather wrong, as we could have learned a great deal from them with further tests and examinations. In the testing which we did undertake, we found traces of Yersinia Pestis on all the bodies discovered, with the exception of one of them: the body which I discovered, and firmly believe to have been that of a doctor. Officially we don't know anything about who any of the dead were, as the parish records did not provide the necessary details, and we probably never will now, sadly.

I have tried speaking with Mr Thurlow and Mrs Johnson, and strongly advised them that if they intend to continue building on the site, the ground should be consecrated beforehand, and the site checked for any further traces of the bacteria. I don't know whether or not my advice will be heeded, seeing as Mr Thurlow was more concerned about time being lost on the construction work than anything else.

I get the impression that certain 'discussions', shall we say, have been had, as the university doesn't seem too concerned about pushing for further investigation either. Maybe all involved feel that there is more to be gained by doing no more research, and that the burial of the bodies offers the closure sought, with the whole affair being swept under the carpet, as it were. Selfishly - from a personal point of view - I must admit that I do ask myself this: who am I to question the decisions made, when my own torment seems to have ceased, now that the bodies have been dealt with and everyone seems keen to move on?

15th *July 1955*

I enclose a letter which I received today from one of the school children (it had been forwarded on to me by Mrs Johnson) who had seen me when I collapsed outside the school that afternoon, on the 22nd, and had obviously been rather worried about me. It was written by the child in their own handwriting, which I find to be rather touching, although the final sentence does deliver a chill like a punch to the gut, somewhat.

The letter is included and reads as follows:

Dear Mister,

I hope you are feeling much better now after you fell over outside our school when we were playing.

From Janet, AGE 9.

PS. That man in the mask who was behind you was very scary. Why did he look like a big bird with a horrible beak, who was standing up and staring at you?

***

As you have seen, this was quite a remarkable account. Upon revealing my findings to the current Group Scout Leader, who was unaware of the events surrounding the Scout Hut's construction, I was asked for discretion, as I suspect that its reveal may have led to some rather awkward questions, hence why I have blocked out locations and altered names. Additionally, I suspect that it may also be prudent to omit the events described above from my final project. For my own curiosity, I have since tried to get in touch with those involved or who knew those involved, to see if anybody can shed any light upon the events described in the journal but have so far been unsuccessful in uncovering further details. The University was certainly aware of Mr Athelstan's work here and acknowledged as such, but declined to comment beyond that, and it very much seems as though there has been a 'hushing up' of the discovery at the site in 1955, with people either knowing little or nothing about it, or not wanting to disclose anything at all. The seeming lack of further investigation into the site and what was found, as well as the speed to which the bodies were subsequently reburied, suggests that apart from Athelstan himself in his journal, nobody involved at the time or indeed since, has been prepared to ask further questions about any of the events, probably as it would likely have been inconvenient, costly, time consuming, and uncomfortable. It should also be noted that Athelstan didn't offer any official protestations against this approach either.

I couldn't tell you whether or not the ground upon which the Scout hut now resides was indeed consecrated on Athelstan's suggestion, but I would not be remotely surprised if he was ignored. I do know, however, that there is a small, discreet memorial somewhere in the local Church grounds to the victims of the 1665 epidemic, and I am told that the bodies which were found during the works were indeed reburied there.

Athelstan seemed much troubled throughout a large portion of what he described, and despite him seemingly finding some relief once his nightmares ceased, I do wonder if he suffered any long lasting effects from his experiences, and I do hope that he was able to access the help that he sought. I believe that he left University College several years later, and in a cruel twist of fate, died after contracting Ebola during an epidemic, whilst doing charity work in Africa in the 1970's.

As to how the journal found its way into the time capsule, we can only speculate, but my guess is that Athelstan may well have been trying to warn of the dangers of interfering where it may not have been best to do so, and he had concerns about what else may lay hidden around the site, yet to be uncovered. It is possible that he requested (or indeed insisted) it be included in the capsule (without revealing what he had written inside it), in the hope that whilst no further action was going to be taken at the time, it may have been in the future.

Apparently, the local council have been keen to acquire the land in recent times, with a view to building new flats on it. Of course, after reading what we have, certain questions could be raised, although I don't expect that if this situation were to come about, that they would be dissuaded by a journal telling of strange goings-on which may or may not have happened to someone over 60 years ago.

And finally, what are we to make of the child's letter at the end of the account? Although Athelstan doesn't comment on it at great length, it does possibly vindicate his thoughts and writings. Does it suggest that Athelstan's dreams, visions, experiences, or whatever you wish to call them, were not just the mere imaginings of someone who had become psychologically unstable, but were, in fact, something more real?

Three Urban Legends of the Scout Troop

I don't believe in ghosts. I would like to inform you of that as an opening statement. I am one of those people who, when it comes to ghosts, or indeed anything pertaining to the supernatural, requires hard evidence or needs to witness something myself before believing. That isn't to say that ghosts, demons, monsters, and the like, are of no interest to me, because they are - after all, I am a writer of tales (or should I say, relater of events) which tend to include them - but I usually see the supernatural as a vehicle to be used purely for entertainment purposes. Despite in recent years enjoying events such as a ghost tour of the Museum of London Docklands, and a Ghost Bus tour around the streets of London, I find myself questioning their validity when it comes to the fact – their value as fiction, I am more certain of.

Despite this scepticism, I do enjoy a good ghost story and have read many of them, finding those by the master, M. R. James, to be superlative. Not only have James' tales inspired me, but I have also drawn on people I have met, places I have been to, and stories I have been told whilst out and about, in writing my own tales.

I began writing these when I was in the Scouts, sharing a ghost story every Christmas in the troop newsletter, which I was also editor of. Scout Monthly, as it was called, featured numerous articles reporting on activities we had done, Scouts' achievements and other noteworthy events, as well as puzzles and games, and other entertaining titbits – which is where the ghost stories would feature. I felt that I was carrying on something of a tradition, as when I was younger, we used to tell ghost stories whilst on camp in the evenings, sometimes sitting around a fire, or at other times huddling inside our tent with the only relief from the dark being a single, unremarkable torchlight. These stories would usually be told by the leaders or older Scouts and would involve a monster or some other form of horror lurking in the bushes of the campsite, waiting to emerge and get us when we were not expecting it.

Many of the stories from those times have become lost, but I would like to share with you now, three urban legends, which I came across during my time in Scouting and which did make an impression. Of course, I find them to be nothing more than entertaining fiction. Those who told them, to their credit, did an admirable job in making them seem as real and believable as possible, and I hope that I can replicate their success here. You must judge for yourselves what you make of them.

I: An Extra Scout

The Group Scout Leader was a marvellous teller of stories, often regaling everyone with anecdotal tales of former Scouts, leaders, and various happenings that he had encountered over his many years of running the troop. More often than not, the stories revolved around the troop's summer camps, which would usually take place at various locations in the opening week of the summer holidays. All who listened heard of Scouts not washing for a full week and being frog-marched down to the shower block as a result, standing under water so cold it could have come directly from the North Sea – the dirt draining off them and the muddy water cascading across the floor of the showers like a tsunami; of other Scouts smuggling food into their tents and keeping it there, opened and expiring in the heat, attracting swarms of ants or intuitive foxes who inevitably invaded; and of various other characters who would leave their mark in some way - often with unusual or hilarious results - during their time away with the troop.

I, myself, was witness to various memorable characters and moments similar to those above, in my time as a Scout. One that I recall, involved a young lad who drank a full litre bottle of Irn Bru in the space of 20 minutes on the way back from Scotland after being told mischievously, that he would not be allowed to take it through the non-existent border control with England. The same Scout had been on the receiving end of another prank earlier in the week, having been sent on a fool's errand to collect various ridiculous and imaginary items from the storage tent such as tartan-coloured paint, fog-locker, skyhook, and left-handed screwdriver. Although on the face of them, the pranks seemed rather cruel, it should be pointed out that everything was done in good spirit, with the Scout in question appreciating the joke, seeing it as some kind of initiation ceremony through which he gained others' respect.

Despite the cruel nature that the Scouts could display to each other on occasion, it should be noted that when in their patrols and working together - each of them bonding and looking out for one another - they were superb, formidable teams. Throughout a week's camp, patrols would compete against each other to win points for the standard of their camping, cleanliness, success in activities, and other criteria, with a winning patrol declared at the end of the week, with a similar points competition running during the regular meetings of the rest of the year.

At the time in question, Panthers patrol was the dominant force, in the same way that certain clubs dominate in football. What annoyed the other patrols was that Panthers always seemed to win, and with ease, despite the best efforts to dethrone them – and it should be said that each of these other patrols were outstanding in their own right – in fact it got to the point where the question was being asked as to what their secret was, as surely there would be one. The answer to the conundrum came from one of the Scouts of the rival patrols, and was this:

"Well, of course they always win…they've got an extra person, haven't they!" It was quite some claim – indeed, complaint – and seemed a strange one, as each of the patrols had the same number of members. The leaders certainly found it perplexing - if you asked the troop to fall-in to a horseshoe formation and inspected them, you would see that with a full house of Scouts, there would be exactly six members in each patrol – and were not aware of any-one having joined that had not been registered. The Scout, how-ever, was adamant that Panthers had an 'extra' member, and their suggestion was also independently corroborated by other Scouts, although those in the Panthers patrol strongly denied the accus-ation – not that the other Scouts believed them, of course. When asked to describe the 'extra' Scout that they saw, they all gave the same description (in my words, not theirs) of a young boy with a cheeky, mischievous manner about him, but with an appearance that was 'ill-defined'. He moved, they added, rather awkwardly as if limping due to some foot injury.

Unlike the Scouts, none of the leaders had had any sighting of this extra Scout, and to begin with, dismissed their claims, but as time went on, they began to reassess their stance, as strange oc-currences took place. On one occasion, a visitor to the headquar-ters commented that they had felt an unusual coldness and some 'presence' there; the description they gave of this 'presence' being that of a young, mischievous boy. Then, some kitchen utensils seemingly disappeared into thin air, before magically reappearing in the kitchen a week or so later, during the clearing-up after an event. This was then followed on another occasion by keys also disappearing during the week; the keys in question were used to open the windows of the building in order to allow ventilation – and of course, their disappearance coincided with a long, hot, July heatwave. Eventually the keys turned up again at the end of a meeting one Friday night in an unexpected location, the very week that the weather turned much cooler and wetter.

Of course, it could be argued that these incidences were all just 'one of those things', with the items simply being mislaid, but it did begin to seem as if some unseen trickster were playing pranks on the troop, in a similar manner to those described earlier. The Scouts were in no doubt as to the cause of the disappearances, and the narrative emerged of the ghost of a boy – who was the extra Scout that had been seen - hiding things at the most inconvenient moments, usually at times when they were required, before teasingly returning them much later.

It is likely that the Group Scout Leader had begun to suspect that the Scouts had not been jesting when speaking of the extra Scout and a final, perhaps more terrifying clue seemed to act as some form of confirmation for him. This final clue was discovered by a small group of Scouts who were being taught axe and saw skills outside, in the grounds of the headquarters one Friday evening. What they found, lying in the grass, was a long, rusted metal nail, covered in blood and the remnants of what appeared to be human flesh. It was a horrifying sight, especially as the impression was given that, despite the nail being of significant age, it had only very recently impaled whatever part of the body into which it had been inserted – in fact it was suggested that the nail looked as though it had been removed shortly before the Scouts had discovered it. A connection was subsequently made, and again, blame was attributed to the extra Scout, and at this point, those in the Panthers patrol finally admitted that they too were aware of the 'presence'.

The Group Scout Leader decided that it was now time tell another story, that of a young lad who had been a Scout at the troop some 20 years previously, as a member of the Panthers patrol. He had been a cheeky, mischievous boy, with a carefree attitude and an unwillingness to listen to instructions - character traits that sadly, would ultimately lead to his downfall. Apparently, he had been up to no good one afternoon whilst on summer camp, acting foolishly and climbing atop a woodpile of wooden crates and other wooden debris, wearing inappropriate footwear. Although dangerously careless, he had been unlucky, as it was surely a huge misfortune to step on a piece of wood that snapped so easily, plunging his foot straight down and through a long, rusted metal nail sticking upwards from out of another piece of wood below it. He was taken to hospital, where the nail was removed from his foot, and he was treated for infection, and although he recovered, he never returned to Scouts, with the Scout Association being sued for negligence. Little was known of what became of the boy after that, although the Group Scout Leader was aware that he had passed away at a relatively youthful age.

It was therefore concluded that Panthers patrol's extra member was in fact the ghost of this boy, and that he had returned, to continue his Scouting. Unlike the Scouts, the adults had still not seen this extra Scout directly, certainly not in his current form, perhaps because he was trying to hide from them. The Group Scout Leader had been deeply sceptical of the whole affair at first, but the descriptions of the boy that the Scouts had given did seem to fit with the boy he had known all those years ago, first planting the seed of doubt into his mind. The disappearances of utensils and keys were now, it seemed, clearly pranks, whilst the metal nail in the grass had been used as an attention grabber, the meaning of which only he knew. As a result, he decided to grant permission for the boy to come back, and with that, it was as if both he and the boy found solace.

As time passed, there became a general acceptance of this extra member of the troop. Any new members of the troop were told the story of the boy when they joined; whilst some of them were sceptical and thought the rest of the troop to be mad, deciding instead to take their Scouting elsewhere, others embraced it, thinking it to be strange, but in some ways, rather 'cool'. The extra Scout was treated like any other member of the troop, having fully integrated with the other Scouts, and it is likely that he is still there today, eternally a member of Panthers patrol and always causing some mischief or other.

II: A Canal Story

One summer, a troop of Scouts hired a narrowboat to sail along the Stratford-upon-Avon Canal. Setting off from the town of Evesham, they travelled along the River Avon, stopping overnight at the idyllic Stratford-upon-Avon, before stocking up on supplies the following morning, then joining the canal and continuing out into the open countryside beyond.

They made good progress on this second day, aided by the fact that they encountered very few stoppages en route, and their day's journey eventually came to an agreeable end when they moored up for the night just past a cast iron aqueduct - having passed over a minor road, suburban railway line, and track bed of a disused railway below it. The weather was fine and warm, and with the longer evening sunshine, they were able to sit outside along the bank of the canal, eating, talking, and relaxing. Seema, who was one of the young leaders, was a fine singer-guitar player, and she entertained them through the evening with traditional campfire songs. The Scouts raucously joined in - and so lively were they, that to any who would have passed by them, the atmosphere conveyed would have been one of a group of youngsters who were in good spirits, carefree and ready for adventure.

It was the following morning, just after breakfast, when the peculiar occurrences which are of interest to us here, began. Kris, the youngest member of the troop, spotted it first: a barge emerging from out of the early morning mist as it began to clear, approaching from the direction in which they were heading. Normally an occurrence such as this would have stirred little interest, as the passing of barges heading in the opposite direction was common, but there was something odd, rather unnatural about this barge, with its monochrome colour scheme and undefined, almost blurry outline, as well as the strange lifeless man dressed in waistcoat and flat cap at the helm. They all stared with astonishment, as it seemed to glide gracefully and noiselessly, in the manner of something travelling in some kind of vacuum without sound, and they felt its strange and somewhat disturbing aura as it got nearer and then travelled past them. It somehow had a transfixing quality about it, as if daring anyone who saw it to ignore its presence, but after a few moments, this power was overcome by the distraction caused by a sudden, and attention drawing sound of a splash. Their collective gaze turned towards the sharp sound that they had heard, only to see Kris holding up his hands in admittance to having been the culprit, having clumsily dropped a saucepan he had been washing into the canal. A couple of the others attempted to assist him as he struggled to retrieve it, but to no avail - as it had drifted too far away from them – however, the moment of clumsiness had proven to be a significant enough distraction as, by the time they had returned their attentions to the barge, it had gone. At first, they were baffled by the episode; the barge itself had been unlike any of the other boats they had encountered thus far, whilst the helmsman had also had an unusual manner and appearance. Quite where it had disappeared to was also a mystery, as it seemed to have vanished into thin air, and it was as if it had never been there at all. They were unable to dwell on the matter at great length as a certain amount of progress needed to be achieved within the day, and so with time not a luxury to them, their thoughts returned to their early morning chores onboard the narrowboat, and then turned to the journey ahead.

As they continued along the canal that morning, the troop had been split into two groups, with Rob and Kris and a few of the others remaining on board the narrowboat, with everybody else - Sam and Seema included - walking alongside on the towpath, ready to open and close any locks that they should come across. Opening and closing the locks would be arduous work, and so those on board would prepare the food for the day and keep the narrowboat clean and tidy, with the roles being reversed every couple of days, a pattern that would run through the week. They went at a steady, but gentle pace, with the main leader acting as helmsman, with Colin, another leader also on board, looking after the mooring ropes, whilst a third leader, Paul, supervised the opening and closing of the locks.

Later in the afternoon they reached a lock, beside which, stood a modestly sized cottage. There was a small, tidy display of memorabilia outside - the various items painted in the colourful and flowery Roses and Castles style canal art. Curious, Sam went to have a look while the troop waited for a boat to use the lock before them, and discovered it to be a souvenir shop selling painted wooden stools, metal watering cans, horseshoes, and the like. A small, unobtrusive sign in the window included mention of a Mrs Jordans, and Sam assumed that she was the shopkeeper - and by the look of the cottage, that she also lived there. As he continued to browse, an elderly woman – stocky, bent over, and dressed in a dark grey dress with knitted shawl about her shoulders - limped out from the entrance door to the cottage and spoke to him.

"You like anything in particular, young man?" she asked, startling Sam, whose back had been turned towards the entrance as he browsed. After a few moments, he regained his composure.

"Not really" he replied, assuming that she was Mrs Jordans.

"Where have you come from?" was the next question, "I haven't seen you around here before". He briefly told her the narrative of who they were and recounted their journey so far. At the mention of the strange barge that they had seen earlier that morning, her whole manner changed, from that of curiosity about the new strangers to one of genuine concern.

"You've seen the barge?" she enquired, with a hint of fear in her voice, and she tried to grab his arm, as if hastily desiring an answer from him as a matter of great urgency. Puzzled, and backing away from her, Sam confirmed that they had, with a questioning frown having appeared on his forehead.

"Lord protect your souls" she said, signing herself with a cross.

"Excuse me?" Sam replied, becoming exasperated by what was turning into a quite extraordinary encounter.

"Oh, if you've seen that barge", she continued, "why, it's trouble, that's what it is...it means no good to anyone who comes across it along here, ever since......." She stopped, seemingly on the brink of revealing significant information to him, and he wanted her to continue, but instead, she became evasive, as if trying to avoid having to clarify her words or answer any of his questions. She then frantically started scrabbling about herself, picking up random painted objects that had been on display for sale, offering them to him. Sam now felt very uncomfortable, and politely refused, stepping back further away from the strange old woman, believing that she was trying to scare him into spending money.

"Please, they will protect you" she pleaded, almost begging him to accept at least one of the items, but he was having none of it and firmly walked away. As he did so, she continued to sign herself with the cross, a look of grave concern etched on her face given in the direction of Sam and the rest of the troop. On his return to the others, Sam said little of his interaction with the strange Mrs Jordans, telling them that the cottage would be of no interest to them and that it was not worthwhile them paying a visit.

Eventually the troop gained access to the lock, and having made their way through it, they then continued along the canal. As they did so, Sam tried to forget about his encounter with Mrs Jordans, but her words kept on floating around inside his head.

"If you've seen that barge...why, it's trouble, that's what it is... it means no good to anyone who comes across it". The words, together with the look of concern on her face, as well as the panic with which she then acted towards him, seemed to foretell some form of impending doom, and the earlier sighting of the strange barge added to an uneasy feeling that grew within him, despite his attempts at dismissing it all as ridiculous.

As they came to another lock, they again had to pull over to the canal bank and moor up, to allow another narrowboat to come through the lock from the opposite direction. As they waited, he sat on the canal bank - his legs dangling over the side - and peered into the water. After a few moments, Sam suddenly saw something that startled him: a pair of eyes, brown he thought, staring back at him from under the water. It wasn't a reflection that he was looking at – he was quite certain of that - because they were clearly not his own eyes, as his were blue, but somehow, he recognised them. Leaning slightly further forward, he tried to get a closer look, but within a matter of moments, they had gone. He stared a little longer, whilst the others called to him, and as he straightened himself back up again and began to stand, he pondered as to whether he had imagined the entire scene. Surely, he thought to himself, there couldn't possibly be anybody under the water, staring back up at him in that moment, as if there were, then they would be….. He abruptly halted his thoughts, partly because he was not keen on where he was going with them, but also as a result of being drawn back to the rest of the group.

The rigours of the day in navigating and working on a canal allowed Sam to keep his mind busy, active, and focused. As they continued along the canal, they admired some beautiful countryside; there were open fields with small dwellings dotted around here and there, as well as more wooded areas with trees overhanging the water. The weather was very warm, and in the perfect summer sunshine, the water glistened peacefully, and every now and then, a large dragonfly would be seen hovering above the surface. Occasionally they would pass hikers with their dogs, walking along the towpath; men fishing by the side of a basin; and small groups of friends sitting on a patch of grass in their green foldable chairs around a tiny barbeque, drinking, laughing, and enjoying the sun.

That evening, Sam was happy. Good food, music, and company kept his mind occupied, but once he had turned in for the night, and his mind became inactive, his thoughts inevitably returned to the strange events of the day, and these thoughts also invaded his dreams too. In his dream, he 'awoke' and found himself lying on top of their narrowboat, as if he had been lying there in the sun, except that it was now dark and misty, and clearly night-time. He looked up and about him with a growing fear as, although the scene seemed still and calm at first, he became aware that something was approaching from out of the mist, and he again heard Mrs Jordans' voice inside his head, saying to him the all too familiar words.

"If you've seen that barge, why, it's trouble, that's what it is…it means no good to anyone who comes across it". He knew what was coming, and sure enough, it was indeed the barge, which they had seen earlier in the day that emerged, helmed by the strange, lifeless man. As it passed, the man turned his head slightly, and although he didn't see a face, Sam knew that it was staring at him. Suddenly he found it difficult to breathe. The man pointed towards the lock by which the troop had moored up for the night, and as the scene changed, Sam realised that the reason he couldn't breathe was that he was now underwater and drowning. He could see the surface above him, but despite his best efforts, he just couldn't reach it and couldn't kick himself upwards, and so it slipped further and further away from him as he sank deeper into the abyss. To make matters worse, he could feel that something had grabbed hold of his ankles and was pulling him down. What it was that had grabbed him, he couldn't tell, but whatever it was it felt like a hybrid of hands and tentacled claws. He tried to scream for help, but doing so only allowed water to pour into his lungs, worsening his situation even further. As it seemed that his end was nigh, the scene disappeared and he awoke for real. Believing himself to be choking, he gasped frantically for air, coughing, and spluttering in a desperate attempt to clear his airways of canal water but thankfully, there was no water there. He found himself to be in his bunk inside the narrowboat, and he realised right away that, despite the seeming reality of what he had just endured, it had been nothing but an awful nightmare.

The following day, every time they approached a lock, Sam had a feeling of trepidation, and this feeling grew as they approached a staircase (a series of locks one after the other, going up an incline). It had been a very humid day and a storm, which had been brewing during the afternoon, finally hit them once they reached the third lock, taking them by surprise. The main leader, at the helm of the narrowboat, began to raise his voice as he issued instructions, while Seema, along with Paul - who had taken charge on the canal bank - were trying to get the others together to operate the locks. Sam felt strange and expectant of something, but he wasn't sure of what. Then, out of the corner of his eye, he noticed that emerging from out of the lock was the barge - the same barge they had seen previously - which seemed to haunt his world in both reality and in his dreams. He wasn't the only person to see it then, but somehow, only he seemed to know what it meant. Mrs Jordans' words came to him once more as the strange helmsman on the barge pointed towards them, and Sam began to have flashbacks to his dreams.

Suddenly, a scream pierced the air, and this was followed by the sound of a splash and then by commotion. Kris had fallen in whilst trying to return to the narrowboat from the towpath, unaware that it was in fact moving away, and despite being a very good swimmer, he had fallen deep down into the water and was struggling to return to the surface. It acted like a trigger point for Sam, bringing him back to the real world from out of his flashback, and instantly, without thinking, he knew what he had to do. He ran over to where Kris had gone in, threw himself to the ground and reached over the side.

Kris was completely submerged, and flailed wildly under the water, struggling to fight his way back up to the surface. For Sam, it seemed as though time stood still as he peered into the water and shouted to his friend, telling him to use his legs to kick himself upwards, all the while reaching into the water but unable to grab hold of anything. Sam could see Kris' brown eyes staring back at him from under the water, just as he had seen them, he realised, the day before, their expression pained and terrified. As Paul came over to help, Kris was briefly able to lift his hands out of the water, but before Sam or Paul could grab a hold of them, they were gone again. Together the pair of them reached into the water once more, desperately trying to save him, but Kris was always just out of reach, and it seemed as if he was being dragged downwards by something that had grabbed his feet, pulling him further away from them and towards his doom.

Suddenly, although they didn't know where it came from, they found an extra 'something' – call it another gear, divine intervention, good fortune, a superhuman effort, or whatever – and they finally managed to reach far enough under the water and were able to grab hold of Kris' arms, before hauling him out of the canal, just in the nick of time. As they did so, Sam glimpsed, or thought he glimpsed, what appeared to be something letting go its' grip of Kris' legs, as if admitting defeat in a contest of tug of war. Quite what it was that he may have seen, he couldn't tell, but he was most certainly reminded of what he had 'felt' grabbing him during his own vision the previous night. Thankfully, Kris emerged from the water conscious, albeit gasping, and had not taken in a huge amount of water, coughing up and spitting out any that he had, before eventually being able to breathe normally, without any need of assistance. The rest of the troop abandoned their tasks and came over to assist, oblivious to the fact that the strange barge with its helmsman had, on the instant of Kris' rescue, simply vanished.

Kris was helped back on board the narrowboat and was taken care of by one of the first aiders. Naturally, he was shaken by the ordeal, but the only physical damage had been a cracked tooth, and with no other emergency assistance required, he had, it seems, been very fortunate. Although to those directly involved in the incident, it had seemed as if time had somehow stood still with Kris' fate in the balance, he had in fact, only been in the water for mere moments.

Sam's dreams and visions were dismissed as a child's imagination, as was Kris' claims of something having grabbed him from below, whilst he had been in the water. As for the strange barge and its helmsman, there were no further sightings of it for the remainder of the troop's voyage. In fact, there may be a solution to the mystery surrounding it, as a possible link has since been made to an accident involving a barge of similar description on the canal in the early years of the 20th century, which had claimed the lives of all involved. Of course, it would be pure speculation to suggest that the barge seen by the Scouts had been the same one, but Mrs Jordans clearly seemed to think it was, and it could be that in the years since, it had been acting to those on the water as a warning of danger to come. While the troop had, it seems, been marked out for catastrophe, they had been able to prevent it, thanks to Sam heeding the warnings and acting upon them; sadly, over the years, others hadn't been as lucky as Kris, as there had apparently been several incidents of people drowning along that stretch of the canal.

Kris recovered from the shock of the incident, as did Sam, although some of the Scouts teased Kris about falling in, and cruelly, albeit somewhat jokingly, warned him of the dangers of Weil's disease. As mentioned, the rest of the trip passed without further notable incident. On the return journey, Sam determined that he would stop at the cottage by the lock and speak again with Mrs Jordans, to ask her some further questions about the canal, the barge, and the trinkets that she had been offering to him as if they were a good luck charm to fend off danger. However, no trace of Mrs Jordans could be found at the cottage (which on this occasion, appeared as if it hadn't been occupied in a long time) – a fact that probably wouldn't have come as a surprise to anybody who knew anything of the history of the local area, seeing as she had been a prominent character in its story. You see, by the time of Sam's encounter with her, Mrs Jordans had been dead for nearly 60 years.

III: Reds versus Greens

Back in the mid to late '90s, laser quest, or Quasar as it was commonly known, became very popular as a fun, interactive activity, especially with youth groups. It was essentially a pain-free version of paintballing, with two teams battling it out for supremacy around an indoor arena, hunting down and shooting at each other using infrared laser rifles.

Each game would last 20 minutes, with participants being split into Red and Green teams, both of which had their own base headquarters – their priority being to successfully attack the other's base, whilst also defending their own. Points would be accumulated on a team and individual basis, with the team collecting the most points being the victors. For those playing the game, it was also the aim, on an individual level, to be named as 'Top Gun', by claiming the most strikes on the opposition's base and the most enemy hits. The more members of the opposite team that a player would shoot, the more points they collected, whilst being shot by others or accidentally shooting members of their own team would result in points being deducted. The opposition's base could be 'bombed', whilst groupings of players could be taken out all at once with a 'grenade' (although this did run the substantial risk of 'friendly fire'), and it would be at the discretion of each of the players how they used the arsenal at their disposal within the rifles, all the while, also weighing up the risk to themselves.

Despite first impressions suggesting an unsavoury, violent activity, Quasar was fun, friendly and harmless. It was an exercise in teambuilding, logical and tactical thinking, as well as good physical exercise, and was perfect for youth groups, Scout troops and the like.

The Scout troop to who this urban legend pertains were regulars at their nearest Quasar venue in South East London, as it was a popular, favourite and much-requested activity with the children. Whilst not an especially large troop, it was still of a decent size nonetheless, and as a result, when they visited the venue, they tended to book entire games out for themselves, with the troop usually being split in half for each game. Occasionally, other participants would join in too, being distributed between the two teams accordingly, with the troop dominating, in terms of numbers. To make an outing worthwhile, two games would be played, with an interval between them for everyone to rest and procure refreshments – which would usually consist of crisps, chocolates, and sugary brightly coloured drinks - the teams then swapping colours for the second game, before heading home at the end of the evening.

The purpose of this narrative is to detail one particular occasion when something went very wrong, on what would prove to be the troop's final visit to the venue. Everything was as normal upon arrival; the Scouts had travelled to the venue in their minibus and changed out of their uniforms – which had been worn during the journey for insurance purposes – into more appropriate attire, before disembarking and making their way inside. As they did so, there was no indication that anything was amiss, and yet their opening game that evening would be abandoned approximately midway through – the reason for this abandonment being most peculiar and still much debated upon even to this day.

As was usual, the troop was split into two teams for the game (or as near as possible, seeing as they were of an odd number), with half of the troop forming the Red team, and the other half being the Green team. The teams were given their equipment, which consisted of a laser gun for each player as well as a colour coded plastic body armour vest. Both items were reasonably heavy, with assistance being required in putting on the vest and then fastening it at the side. Each gun was numbered - with the vest corresponding to it - the number displayed being that player's identification for the game. The vest itself was styled as a combat garment made of plastic, with large shoulder pads; battery packs were placed on both the front and back of the vest - the packs also containing sensors that would detect any hit from enemy fire - and along with the gun itself, would be the primary targets for the players when shooting at each other. The gun itself featured a strap which allowed it to be worn over the shoulder, with house rules stipulating that the gun must be worn in that way at all times. Once their equipment was received, checked and then in place, they were ready for battle.

Inside the arena, it was very dark, with only intermittent strobe lighting and minimal fluorescent torchlights dotted around to help them see where they were going. Loud techno music played in the background, to give a deafening, oppressive atmosphere, which was heightened by the presence of dry ice. The arena resembled a grim futuristic industrial landscape, similar to that which might be seen in a pulp science fiction film, with obstacles, ramps, and various hiding places being scattered around, making it ideal for guerrilla urban warfare.

The game commenced as soon as they entered the arena. Upon entering, they needed to head straight to team base in order to charge their weaponry (which could be a slow, arduous process with everyone having to use the same charging booth) before heading out into combat - all the while vulnerable to immediate attack from their adversary. Reds would shoot Greens and vice versa, and sometimes the players would accidentally shoot members of their own team in the ensuing chaos. If they were shot, the players would feel their equipment vibrate and an alert would tell them in a robotic computerised voice "DEFENCE SHIELD ACTIVE...WARNING! WARNING!" As a result, they would be unable to fire back for several moments as their gun would be 'frozen', leaving them vulnerable to repeated attacks by the same player and others, making it vital that they find cover and hide. In the event of needing to return to base to re-energise their gun once it had lost power, they would be even more open to attack as they were not afforded any respite.

The more cautious among the players would usually become engaged in and bogged down by tactical, cat-and-mouse style ongoing battles with others, whilst the more attack-minded players were more likely to make bold moves against the enemy's base, sometimes going on what could be described as reckless 'suicide missions', although both running and physical combat were prohibited. In whichever way the players were involved in the game, the Scouts usually thoroughly enjoyed themselves and expended a good deal of energy.

The colours of the teams were very distinctive, and as the body armour vests had a luminescence to them, it was relatively easy to tell who was on the Red team and who was on the Green team, even in the dark. Yet, as the game progressed, many of the Scouts were becoming increasingly bemused, with there being one question of significance: who exactly were the Blue team? It had been clear to the Scouts as they had entered the arena that only two teams would be playing the game: a Red team and a Green team. But a number of the Scouts had noticed that a third team, carrying the same equipment as them and wearing identical body armour vests were also participating. This third team's vests had the same luminescence, but with a noticeable blue colour, however due to the lack of proper lighting in the arena, little could be discerned of their appearance beyond their body outlines. These other players had started appearing individually or in small groups, sporadically throughout the arena, seemingly emerging randomly and out of nowhere, running around and shooting at everybody – anybody – they encountered before disappearing again, and were becoming something of a nuisance.

A little way beyond the 11th minute mark, one of the Scouts who was playing on the Green team found themselves ambushed by members of the Red team whilst attempting to attack their base, and upon being shot multiple times, found it necessary to retreat and find somewhere to hide for a few minutes, to wait for their gun to 'un-freeze'. They found for themselves a fine place to hide, behind some oil drums in one of the darker recesses of the arena, crouching down and remaining alert. As they waited, they took the time to compose themselves and rest, occasionally peering out from behind the drums with appropriate caution, with the intention of re-emerging when it would be safe to do so.

At first, they felt quite safe there, hidden away behind the oil drums, but suddenly, that reassurance gave way, and a feeling of unease crept upon them, with a suspicion that another player was there, with them in that hiding space. It seemed quite ridiculous at first, as the space appeared to be so small that there seemed to be only just enough room for one person, never mind another as well – but that feeling of having someone else there with them was growing, and was no longer just a suspicion but a realisation, as an uncomfortable and oppressive dread started to weigh down upon them. In turning around, to see what was behind them, they somehow knew that not only was there someone else there in the darkness, but that it would be someone who they wouldn't know. Although in reality there was little point in trying to communicate above the high noise level in the arena, the Scout shouted a frantic and terrified enquiry into the darkness.

"Hello? Is someone there?" Unsurprisingly there was no audible response, but instead the reply was a physical one, as the Scout saw movement in the darkness, and the outline of another player beginning to emerge. It was clear, however, from the glow that was emanating from this other player as they revealed themselves ever more, that they were neither a member of the Red team or the

Green team, for the colour of their glow was blue. The Scout saw that they too had the same equipment as everyone else, with the exception being the armoured vest, which was identical in every way, apart from the colour. However, it was not just their vest, but their entire complexion which appeared to be bright blue, as their face, neck, hands, and eyes all had an extraordinary and over-powering glow to them, making it seem that there was very little, if anything, that was human about them!

In examining this other player, the Scout froze in a terrified amazement at the sight that was now before them, as the Blue team member had finally been fully revealed. They found themselves gazing into its blue face, unable to pull away their attention, so utterly mesmerised by what they were confronted with, as this other's pupil-less eyes stared fixedly back with a sinister emptiness that could have only intended malice towards anyone who looked into them. As they stared, somehow this face and these eyes caused a burning sensation across the Scout's own face and, screaming in horror the Scout lifted their hands to shield themselves, as it seemed that this being in front of them had the power to destroy them by turning them to charcoal, in the same way that Medusa would turn another being to stone. The Scout summoned the ability to stand and staggered upwards and out of their hiding space, fleeing with a desperate need to escape, but they did so with this other player in pursuit. By now, the Scout was no longer alone in their screams, as many players from both the Red and Green teams ran around panic-stricken, screaming throughout the arena, as this mysterious Blue team had finally emerged from out of the darkness in full force and now ran amok, bringing terror to all they encountered.

The game was stopped immediately, and thankfully, everybody was able to escape unhurt – with the Scout described above not actually having suffered any burns at all - but naturally, in the aftermath, the venue was thoroughly investigated by the authorities. It is important to understand that no physical evidence of any such Blue team was found, and the staff at the venue were just as perplexed as everyone else about the affair. Upon examining the hiding place described above in full light, it was determined that there could only have been enough space for one person, not two, again adding doubt to the claims that had been made. And yet, the statements from all the players involved in the game told of the same thing: a third team, a Blue team, at first appearing intermittently and then running amok.

Security footage filmed before, during, and after the incident, showed that the arena had been totally empty of any players prior to the game, but as it progressed there did appear to be a significant number of what were described as 'indefinite shapes that may have been human-like forms, seemingly flitting in and out of proceedings, but which were clearly not players who had been admitted to the arena for that particular game'. As the footage was examined more carefully, no indication was given as to where they had come from, or indeed where they abruptly disappeared to once the Scouts had fled, and with no hidden entry or exit points having been found anywhere around the arena, no satisfactory explanations to what had occurred could be offered. With no physical evidence of anything untoward having actually taken place, the venue re-opened, although the Scout troop never returned.

Following another identical incident months later, involving different players, the venue gained an unfortunate reputation as a place where 'monsters lurked', despite the same inconclusive verdict in the aftermath as before. Punters stayed away, and with a significant drop in revenue, the venue finally closed for good as it could simply no longer pay its rent. The site has been abandoned since, and the mystery of the Blue team has remained unsolved, with paranormal investigations providing no informative conclusions of any value. Various theories have been put forward as a solution, including an intriguing one that the Blue team were some kind of beings who had been residing at the site for an unknown period of time, but had been disturbed by the Scouts during their game – the fact that the Scouts had visited on a Friday evening and had numbered 13, may, perhaps, have had something to do with it.

PART TWO

Mr Wells and Other Ghosts

On the Subject
of Gargoyles

Now, I must confess, that up until quite recently, I had never heard of Linklaters, and I must thank Lucy Henderson for enlightening me about this strange and fascinating place. It was built sometime in the mid-nineteenth century in the Victorian-gothic style, and having recently seen photographs of the place, I initially thought of it as a vicarage, although I don't believe that this was its purpose. It was built of grey brick, with ivy partially hiding the front of the building; there was a gabled roof of slate tiles; the windows were sash; a small porch was at the front of the property with an arched door; and it was surrounded by grass, shrubbery and a small, narrow gravel path which went around it, with hedges somewhat blocking the view of the outside world. When it was built, it was situated just outside of London, but nowadays lies within its boundaries in an area which is much more urban than the time which it was last inhabited. It is at this point that I should mention that it has been abandoned for over 100 years and left to rot, occasionally occupied by addicts, squatters and others; but what is strange is that no one has resided there for any length of time, and those that occupied it, left by their own free will rather than by force, as if they couldn't get away from the place quickly enough.

I have already mentioned that I first heard about Linklaters from Lucy, a neighbour of mine, who I share a passion for local history with, and who works at the local Library and Archive Studies Centre. She came to hear about the place at a local history day, where she was helping with some of the displays and talking to people about their memories and stories of their local area.

"Excuse me" a voice enquired from behind Lucy as she had her back to them, whilst fixing one of the display boards which had become loose, "you wouldn't happen to have anything on Linklaters, would you, by any chance?" Lucy turned around to face the elderly gentleman who had posed the question.

"My apologies" she replied, hoping that he had not found her to be rude by having her back turned. The gentleman repeated his question, in a tone which confirmed that he had not found Lucy to be rude. As he spoke, Lucy searched her memory but was struggling to recollect ever hearing of any place called Linklaters, and a vague look appeared across her face, indicating that there was unlikely to be anything relating to it on display.

The gentleman continued, "don't worry, very few people know about it, and those that do don't bother to speak about it anymore – I only know of it through my grandfather, who told me the story, and in some ways, I wish he hadn't." Thus started the conversation which led to Lucy learning of the story behind the last occupant of Linklaters, which may, perhaps, give us some reasoning as to why the house has been abandoned ever since and why nobody has had the will-power to simply pull it down.

****

So having provided you with a little bit of background, I shall now relate the story to you, as it was told to Lucy, and then to me, and I believe it to be as complete with regards to details as it is ever likely to be:

Our setting is just before the First World War, around 11 months or so, and the gentleman who occupied Linklaters was a Dr Powell (although, I am afraid to say that I do not know what he was a doctor of). He was a middle-aged educated man, who had recently moved to the area to escape the increasingly hectic London life. The prominent feature of the property, with which Dr Powell was instantly struck, and helped persuade him to choose it, was a gargoyle perched at the top of the gabled roof, at the front of the building. It was an odd-looking thing, made of stone, with the appearance of an emaciated creature similar to a hyena, but with wings attached and an overly long and thin tail, as well as a single horn, significant in length, emerging upwards from the top of its head. It was perched there in an attitude of peering over the edge and watching, waiting, as if ready to leap down upon those it did not approve of; and its face bore a sly, sinister smile with sharp teeth on display. I am sure that to you or I this thing would be repulsive, but to Dr Powell, it was intensely fascinating. He had a passion for architecture, and I am sure that he must have viewed Linklaters as something akin to heaven, so it is perhaps no surprise that he chose to make Linklaters his home, nor would it be a surprise to learn that soon after taking up residency, he began to make an architectural survey of the property, paying particular attention to the aforementioned gargoyle.

It was not long after his arrival, that he first met the local vicar, Reverend Robert Faverstone, and it is at this point that I should probably mention to you that he was the grandfather who passed on this version of events which I am now telling you. The two gentlemen discovered that they had similar interests and they struck up a good friendship, although I suspect that Dr Powell saw an opportunity to use this friendship to gain some knowledge regarding his gargoyle. One morning, the two of them met for a coffee and it was then that Dr Powell took the opportunity to finally enquire after the gargoyle and was particularly interested to discover where it had come from. He was rather surprised, as the normally open and talkative Reverend became rather coy and evasive, and anxious to change the topic of conversation, and although the Doctor continued to press, the Reverend still refused to be forthcoming with information, and so, eventually, Dr Powell admitted defeat.

Our story now moves forward a few weeks to a bright Sunday morning after the early Service. As he departed the church, Dr Powell was called by someone behind him, and on turning around, discovered it be his friend, the Reverend.

"Dr Powell" he began, "you have enquired several times about the gargoyle atop your house, and in particular, regarding its origins……" Dr Powell began to raise his hopes that, at long last, he would finally gain the sought-after information, "…..if you meet me here at 12 o'clock precisely, I shall take you to the place which you're seeking, and which will hopefully provide you with some answers. It is a Sunday, so we will be safe, thank goodness". It was this last sentence which struck the Doctor, and he intended to press the Reverend further as to what he meant by it whilst they were on their expedition - and indeed an expedition it most certainly was; upon meeting outside the church at the appointed time, they proceeded to hike for a couple of miles across open fields and along narrow country lanes.

Their destination was an ancient, ruined Abbey, with access to it being through some very dense hedgerows lining one of the lanes along which they were walking. The Abbey had been destroyed during the Reformation, but previously, its reputation had been an 'unusual' one, with the suggestion being that some of the activities which took place within were not exactly befitting of those of a Holy Order, and that some of the things which were practised, were from the outer reaches of Christian teaching, if not outside of it. It was a reasonably large and grassy site, but now mostly hemmed in by rows of trees. There was still a decent amount of the structure still standing, although most of the walls were no more than a foot or so higher than the grass. The Reverend informed Dr Powell that it was from the Abbey that his gargoyle had been retrieved, having fallen to the ground during the Abbey's destruction, and remained there in the intervening centuries before being collected during the construction of Linklaters. As they explored, the Reverend imparted some of what he knew of its history and layout – I say 'some', because the Doctor was convinced that he was holding things back. He asked his friend if any more of the gargoyles had been found on the ground, to which the Reverend replied that, to his knowledge, there hadn't, but the Doctor wasn't sure that he entirely trusted the answer.

Now, you must understand that at first, Dr Powell experienced nothing untoward at all, and in fact, he continued to live a relatively peaceful existence, but he developed a fascination with the Abbey and in particular, its gargoyles, so much so that he began a detailed study of them, creating a file of sketches and notes, titled 'On the Subject of Gargoyles'. However, in order to carry out his study, he decided that he would need to visit the site again, but when he asked the Reverend to accompany him once more, the man refused flatly and rather bluntly, and seeming flustered, he mumbled something to the Doctor about it not being a Sunday and that it would not be safe, warning him, begging him not to make the journey. The Doctor found it extraordinary that a man of the cloth would seem so perturbed by local superstition, something which of course, to rational men, would be nonsense. His resolve, however, would not fail, and as he remembered the way, he decided to go to the Abbey on his own.

As he marched determinedly to the Abbey through the peaceful countryside, he pondered on the warnings of his friend, dismissively, before his mind wondered onto other things as he enjoyed the pleasant walk. Once he arrived at the site, Dr Powell decided to make a more detailed exploration, hoping to come across something which he not seen before, and on examining one of the taller walls (he assumed it to be an outer wall) which was still standing, he found himself to be 'in luck' as there, perched up high, peering out, was another gargoyle. On the previous occasion, the Reverend had suggested that his theory regarding gargoyles was that they were designed and built to act as guardians, to stop those from entering into a building who should not, with the inference being to evil not being welcome in a place of God – although with the rumours circulating about this Abbey and its history, I would suggest that here it was likely to be more twisted than that. Certainly, the Doctor could see the Reverend's point as, upon staring up at the gargoyle, he did find it to be rather intimidating, and there was something rather dark about it. It was the statue of a man, well he thought it to be a man, but so big and deep did the hooded robes that it was wearing appear to be, that he could not discern any of its actual features, as they were hidden. He felt cold just then, but decided that he must sketch it, and so he found a small lump of stone, which may have been the lower part of a column, sat down and began to sketch. He was there for a long while, looking up from time to time, so that he could sketch as accurately as possible and he did feel at peace – for a time.

As he sat there, he noticed that something about the place had changed. Also, the wind had begun to pick up and rustled more prominently amongst the leaves on the trees - well he thought this was it, but the atmosphere around the site had become such that he couldn't be sure about the wind, as "surely the wind doesn't whisper", he thought, "especially not in Latin!". Whatever the sound was, it seemed to swirl about him, but as he looked towards another part of the Abbey, just to his right, he noticed something move slowly, teasingly behind the wall - something tall, dark, and mysterious. "A figure, perhaps?" he wondered, but that would be a ridiculous suggestion, as he was surely there alone, despite the possibility of voices whispering.

"Is anybody there?" he called out, not expecting to receive an answer, and unsurprisingly, he didn't. He got up, and decided to have a walk around, to see if he could see anybody else there at the site, but he did not. He felt that he had gained what he had wanted from this particular visit, and although he had seen other gargoyles there too, these would require further attention on another occasion, as he didn't feel inclined to linger any longer.

His walk back to Linklaters, although he had been on his own, had not been as pleasant and as peaceful as his outward journey, but once he got home, he seemed to feel safer again. He was satisfied, though, with his afternoon's work and placed his latest sketch, that of the gargoyle of the hooded figure, inside his file of notes and sketches. He stayed up late that evening, writing up a report on his day's findings, before closing the file, with the sketch as the top page, sealing it with string tied in a bow, and left it on his desk in his study. Imagine, then, his surprise, when, on the following morning, he found this file, lying there on the floor in the centre of the room, as if the desk had been disturbed. The Doctor picked up the file and looking at it, it seemed as though no damage had been done. He then tidied the desk, placing the file back where he had left it. He undid the bow tied in the string and opened the file. Another surprise awaited him upon opening it, as he found on the inside cover, to his astonishment, some scratch marks. Quite how they had got there, he couldn't say, but he could definitely confirm that they had not been there when he had closed the file the previous evening. If I could describe the marks to you, I would liken them to the kinds of marks that you might see on the inside lid of a coffin which had housed someone who had been buried despite being not entirely dead, and had been scratching with their fingernails, desperately trying to escape. The sight of these marks disturbed him, and he noticed that sitting there opposite to them, was his sketch of the gargoyle of the hooded figure.

It is from this point onwards, that events began to spiral downwards for Dr Powell. The following night, he was awoken by a light banging sound, and as he lay there in his bed, he decided that it sounded like footsteps and seemed to be coming from above him, possibly from the attic. He lit his lamp, put on his dressing gown and slippers, and made his way up a ladder and through the square hatch into the attic. He shone his lamp to all corners, and it was clear that there was nothing or nobody there which could have made the noise. Then, the banging resumed, and it seemed as though it was, in fact, coming from the roof, but quite why anybody would be on the roof at that hour, or how they would have got up there without assistance in the first place, was a mystery to him. He made his way back down, and then ventured outside.

Again, after shining his lamp and looking around, he could see nobody on the roof, or indeed anywhere around the property.

The next morning, as he was once again examining the property, to check in the daylight that nothing was amiss, he spotted something which he had not seen before: another gargoyle was there, just under the roof guttering, on the front corner of the building. He looked up at it and saw that it was another figure, this time that of a man, although he saw from its features that it had been designed in the style of a hideous caricature with overly-large eyes, and it was wearing garments in the Medieval style. Its facial expression seemed to suggest that it was either screaming, laughing, or mocking – he could not tell which. He frowned at first, but then, thinking it to be an oversight on his part and that he had missed it in his observations, he thought no more of it and continued with his day's activities and research. But, on the following day, his mood changed completely, upon discovering that this new gargoyle was no longer in the spot it had occupied the previous day. Furthermore, he found that it had moved, and was now about a foot lower down than before, and its posture, which had also changed – and this was what disturbed Dr Powell the most – suggested that the gargoyle had been using its arms to creep down the wall! It was the same again the next day when he went to look, for he saw that again it had moved further down, and then the day after too.

I should mention that we know all of this from his file, 'On the Subject of Gargoyles', because inside there were sketches, matching the new gargoyle which I have described, with notes next to them detailing his thoughts. He also recalled within the notes another of the Reverend's theories that gargoyles may have been modelled on actual beings. It is certainly apparent that the Doctor became more and more disturbed as time went on as his language became more irrational, his spelling erratic, and his handwriting deteriorated.

His friend, Reverend Faverstone, became gravely concerned for him, especially when he started missing Sunday services, and decided to pay him a visit. Apparently, he found the Doctor in a bit of a nervous state, rambling on about there having been another 'visitor' earlier that morning. When the Reverend pressed him further, he learnt that Dr Powell had been sitting at his desk after breakfast, when he noticed that the room suddenly got a little darker, as if something was blocking the sunlight coming through the windows. He turned around and swore that there was someone standing there looking through the glass. Startled, he got up to have a closer look, but as he did so, the figure moved. He left his study and saw from the hallway that the figure was now standing by the front door. The Doctor moved towards it and opened the door quickly but found nobody there. He stepped outside and looked first to his right, and seeing nothing untoward, he then looked left, and this time he saw the person, if indeed that was what it was, rounding the corner of the building. This visitor, from the brief glimpse that he had of it, was wearing some form of long, black, woollen, hooded garment, like that of a monk, and was walking slowly, teasingly. The Doctor followed, but once he got to and then looked around that corner, he saw that it had moved quickly, and was rounding the next corner. The Doctor continued to follow but was never able to catch-up with the mysterious visitor, before he finally ended up back at his front door. At first, he thought that he had imagined it, as the visitor seemed to have vanished, but when he looked at his front door, he realised that it had not been his imagination at all, as there, in the centre of it, were scratch marks, similar to those he had found inside his folder – marks, which he was sure, had been made by fingernails, human or otherwise!

At first, the Reverend thought that, perhaps, his friend had had a bad night and that his mind was playing tricks on him, but upon viewing the Doctor's file on gargoyles, and examining its contents, along with the scratch marks inside its front cover as well as those on the door, he found it all disturbingly fascinating and was unable to draw any conclusions which he felt worthy of a man of reason.

On the final day of Dr Powell's residency at Linklaters, he had,

I was told, breakfast as usual, and afterwards sat down at his desk in the study, when there was a knock at the front door. This was accompanied by a voice, which seemed, to the Doctor, to be that of his friend the Reverend. Dr Powell went to open the door, and upon not seeing his friend there, he stepped outside. There was still no sign of the Reverend, and as he turned to move back inside, he noticed that the most recent gargoyle had once again moved, having 'climbed' down the wall to his height level. He moved in closer and saw that the facial expression of the man in stone was more fearful than before. The Doctor stepped back slowly, perturbed by what was before him - it made him feel uneasy, as it appeared to be staring directly at him. Suddenly, he stopped moving backwards, his body suffering a paralysis brought on by fear, as he heard a strange, growling sound from above. His legs weakened and his heart sank as he realised that perhaps the one thing that he had feared most throughout the whole saga was upon him. He looked up and to his horror, his eyes looked upon the original gargoyle, the one which had enticed him to Linklaters in the first place, the one which had been some kind of horrible amalgamation of animal, beast and demon. But now, everything had changed, for it was no longer an inanimate object made of stone, but a living, breathing creature, come to him in that moment from the depths of hell and it was poised, ready to pounce upon him!

I can tell you that Reverend Faverstone, who had been coming to check upon his friend, was the first on the scene, upon hearing the commotion. He is adamant that, on glancing initially through a gap in the hedge at the front of the property, he saw Dr Powell lying on the ground, grappling with something, winged and horned he thought, which was on top of him. Whatever it was that he had seen, it had gone by the time the Reverend reached his friend, who was there, lying on the ground, mumbling and in terrible shock, with, the Reverend later added, a facial expression not too dissimilar from that seen in the Doctor's sketches. Perched above them, on top of the gabled roof, looking down on them from on high, was the original gargoyle, which was, the Reverend noticed, as still and as lifeless as you would expect from something made of stone.

The Doctor was taken away from Linklaters that same day, and I do not know what became of him. I believe that the Reverend and other local men vowed to board up the property, to prevent anything happening to anybody else. As to the presence of the other gargoyles, which, it seems, Dr Powell was the only person to have seen in physical form, I couldn't possibly comment, as I suspect that no-one has ever dared to find out anything more about them.

The Curator
of Radios

The three of us were very good friends. We had met at our place of work and ranged in age from our late 20s through to late 30s and we enjoyed each other's company. We also had the same kinds of interests (photography was the main interest, which had first brought us together), we had fun, and each of us had a quirky sense of humour. An element of playful banter was also involved in our friendship - deriving from recognising and playing upon each other's foibles - and allowed us to bounce off each other perfectly. It could certainly be suggested that as a trio, we were a little eccentric, and those who knew us as a trio often wondered if we were 'up to no good', not in a negative way I might add, but rather like silly schoolboys, laughing at silly things with a hint of immaturity, or getting into unusual scrapes. We called ourselves 'The Chummies' and in some ways, we modelled our adventures on those you might have seen in the Ladybird books of the middle part of the 20th century, or the tales of the Famous Five and other similar books.

We had shift patterns which involved working at weekends,

and so our adventures occurred on days during the week. Often, our trips would be rather unusual: one such outing was to a local airfield and memorial chapel - with what seemed like the world's roughest, bounciest bus journey to get us there and back - where we met a volunteer who probably hadn't spoken to another soul for weeks; another outing involved a hike exploring and photographing the countryside, encountering as we walked 'country folk', who seemed to view us 'town folk from London' with deep suspicion, giving the impression that they might have introduced us to the Wicker Man if they had the chance; and we also had a number of outings to various London museums, including one that focused on childhood - and of course, we inevitably ran into hundreds of schoolchildren on a trip, despite our best efforts to avoid them at all cost.

Out of all our adventures, there is one particular trip that I still remember the most vividly and would like to recall it for you here. As my narrative progresses, it will become clearer as to why it is so well remembered by us, even to this day, and I certainly believe it to be the strangest of all our adventures (or scrapes) so far.

***

It is certainly quite remarkable what you can find whilst bored and with plenty of time on your hands to while away, as you search the internet for anything which may pique a more eccentric curiosity, such as that which the three of us had. The museum that we found whilst browsing certainly fitted the criteria and seemed rather quirky and old fashioned. It was a museum all about vintage radios and televisions and had a simple website, suggesting that it was not likely to be a large, well-funded establishment. This was not unsurprising, as it was clearly the type of place that would only really appeal to those with a niche interest - but nevertheless, although none of us had any particular interest in radios or televisions, it did seem to be just the sort of thing that would be right up our street, as it were. In all honesty we saw it more as a 'bit of laugh', and something silly which we could do and then tell everyone about afterwards as a wacky boy's own adventure, and so we decided to arrange a visit. I must say that it all seemed very legitimate too, and the museum even had a famous broadcaster as a patron, adding to the impression that it would be a place of interest, and for those within the niche, it would be a popular, essential visit.

We booked our appointment for 2 o'clock on a Wednesday afternoon, and provided contact details to the museum via the online booking form, whilst we also made a note of the museum's details for our own reference. The day itself was a warm, humid one - the closeness being a little oppressive – but as we met at the station for our short train journey, we began the day, I think, with pre-conceptions as to what we believed the museum, and indeed the day itself, would be like. I certainly wouldn't describe our anticipation as that of excitement, more that of immature curiosity - we did find it hard to suppress the odd schoolboy giggle when conjecturing as to what we might find upon our arrival at the museum – and I suspect that our 'boyish chatter' did not go unnoticed by those who were in our vicinity on our particular train carriage. Looking back now with hindsight, I can confirm that the museum would prove to be quite different to what we envisaged when setting out that morning.

We found it strange that, on exiting the station after alighting from the train, we could find no directional signs to it or any indications on local information boards that the museum even existed. As is far too typical now at local train stations across the UK, the ticket office was closed, and with no station staff to be found, there was nobody we could ask for further information, and I would say that a niggling concern was beginning to arise. However, an encounter with a younger, trendy couple, who were clearly on their way to some nearby Instagrammable café or some such establishment, provided some light relief.

"Are you lads lost?" the young lady enquired, clearly noticing not only our desperately poor attempts at hiding the fact that we were not local and were evidently seeking directional guidance, but also our awkwardness and reluctance to admit so and ask for assistance.

"Oh, no, we are fine, thank you" we lied, the look of nervous embarrassment in our expressions.

"Actually, we're on our way to the wireless museum!" one of us said, breaking rank in a strange, geekily excited fashion which most likely portrayed us in that moment as oddballs, nerds, and the kind of people that the couple would normally attempt to avoid any form of interaction with. I admit that, in that moment, I wanted to quietly step away and pretend that I had no part in the expedition, but I did feel a need to try to rescue the situation and reverse the perception that the couple now had of us as the biggest nerds with the most peculiar of interests. Sadly, however, I failed.

"Do you know of it?" was all I could say by way of an interjection. I had meant it as a blasé, rhetorical question, with a pretence that I cared little for the answer, but instead, I merely confirmed my involvement. The couple answered, predictably, that they had never heard of the museum, and after a few awkward moments, departed with such haste that clearly, they couldn't wait to get away from us.

As they walked off, the couple were clearly discussing us with disapproval, made clear by the backward glances they gave in our direction - the type of glances that are usually made by those who have had encounters with people they believe to be 'unusual' or a bit 'odd'. Rather than being offended, we actually found it quite amusing and giggled once again, this time at the geeky way we had come across, and we gave ridicule towards my friend who had excitedly declared our destination to the couple that we had encountered. We thought it best to avoid any more interactions with the locals for the time being, so as not to risk revealing our mission and projecting an image of eccentric nerdiness any further. It would be best, therefore, to try to find and locate the museum ourselves.

I must say that the alarm bells began to ring for me once we confirmed the museum's location via Google Maps and then followed its instructions to our destination. Although the app is a wonderful too to have at one's disposal, it can be rather haphazard: not always directing you to the correct place, pointing you in the wrong direction, or taking you on a route which would have been best avoided. After a 25 minute walk, we found ourselves, to our surprise and indeed, dismay, in a South London suburban cul-de-sac, outside a red brick Victorian detached house with a small and unassuming front garden. We stood across the road from the house feeling rather bemused and concerned that we were in fact lost. Quite why we had been directed here was not clear to us, and there was certainly no indication that a museum was nearby, certainly not what would normally be thought of as a museum, anyway. There was an eerie calmness there, with the lack of people disconcerting, as surely, we supposed, there would be other visitors who had come to see the museum, if this was indeed the correct location.

With a hurriedly made a telephone call to the museum, informing them that we appeared to be lost, and that with our appointment time now likely to pass - as we felt that we were clearly too far away from where we believed the museum would be for us to make it in time (despite what Google Maps was telling us) - we had decided that it would be best to reschedule for another occasion. To be brutally honest, I was somewhat relieved that we had come to this decision and wasn't overly disappointed at this turn of events, either. However, to our surprise, we were informed that we were indeed in the correct location, and furthermore, the lady who had taken our call and who was speaking to us confirmed, in a way which made us feel slightly uncomfortable, that not only were we right outside the museum, but that she could also see us standing in the road. Adding to a growing sense of unease regarding our situation, the front door of the house outside which we stood, suddenly creaked open as the lady spoke with us on the phone.

Unsure, and perturbed, we subconsciously debated with each other our next move, and agreed, slightly reluctantly I think, to advance towards the door. For a few moments, nothing happened, and then, slowly, a face appeared from out of the doorway. The face belonged to a middle-aged lady with short fair hair, and in fairness, she seemed rather benign, and dare I say it, friendly, and indeed very welcoming.

"Come in" she said, gesturing excitedly and gratefully towards us to enter, "you must be here for the museum". Our suspicions, which had grown with something of a sinking feeling, had now been confirmed: the museum we had come to see, was not as we had envisaged, and was not a museum in the usual sense, but was in somebody's house. It was also clear that we were the only visitors of the day, and dare I say it, were probably the only visitors that had been there for quite some time.

Once inside, we felt that we had stepped into a house that had been frozen in time at some point in the late 1940s, with the Second World War still fresh in the memory of whoever lived there. It was obvious that there had been little renovation or re-decoration undertaken at the house for several decades, and I think we half-expected to see blackout curtains, tape criss-crossed on the windows, an Anderson shelter in the garden, and ducks flying on the wall. There was a stuffy atmosphere about the place, a smell of mothballs, and a vague feeling of some strange, creeping oppression somewhere in the background. We were ushered down the hallway, and into the living room, and it was here that a most extraordinary sight awaited us, for the room contained dozens and dozens of vintage televisions, many of them clearly some of the earliest ever made, all stacked up on top of each other, seemingly covering every inch of the room. We gazed about us, awe-struck by what we saw, and especially by the scale of the display. The curator had obviously had a life full of collecting, and we had no doubt that he would tell us all about it when we met him, for this clearly didn't seem to be a hobby, but an obsession.

"I shall be back in a moment" the lady informed us, before retreating to another part of the house. While we awaited her return, we looked further about the room. An armchair was in the corner of the room by the window, with a standing lamp next to it as well as a small table, upon which was a hardback book, the subject of which, unsurprisingly, was radios. The chair looked as if it had been well used, and had also been sat upon quite recently, although I did get the impression that it had probably not been occupied by the lady herself, as she appeared to have been undertaking some task in the kitchen before we arrived, as suggested by her clutching a tea towel when she had first spoken to us in person.

Suddenly, and with no warning, there was the sound of a click, followed by a low buzzing and humming sound. Startled, we quickly turned towards the noise and found that one of the television sets had switched on, all by itself. Then another switched on, and another, and rapidly every single television set was switching itself on, one after the other, as if awakened from some kind of slumber. It was a creepy, unnerving experience, and had been totally unexpected, catching us in a moment when, despite us being on our guard, we were still somewhat vulnerable. Again, it felt as though we had wandered into some surreal world where everything had been stuck in a bygone age, with the television screens showing vintage footage from times past. As we watched, we saw black and white children's television programmes, footage of the 1953 coronation, and Steptoe & Son, to name but a few.

"My father gave his heart, soul, mind, everything, to radio and television" said a voice from behind us. We turned around and saw the lady standing in the doorway. She had crept up on us somewhat, and we certainly hadn't heard her return, although this was perhaps unsurprising, so taken aback and distracted by the television sets had we been.

"If you will follow me, I shall take you upstairs to begin our tour" she declared, and I suspect that the three of us were more than happy to start, as we all wanted to get away from this room of television sets. The sets had certainly perturbed us as they seemed to have minds of their own and a penchant for bringing about unease and a creepy sense of something we couldn't quite discern, having provided what you might call a 'jump scare'. As we departed -and I must mention that I was the last to leave the room - I had the impression that the television screens flickered behind us, as if trying to find a path through distortion to something else to display.

The lady took us on a tour around the house and it was certainly a treasure trove, full of televisions, radios, other communication devices, tools, electrical components, and spare parts. As I mentioned, we began by going upstairs, and before climbing, I noticed on the ground floor a room at the back of the house, next to the kitchen. It was behind a door which was closed, and although I only glanced at it briefly, for someone reason it intrigued me, and it certainly gave the impression that it was not going to be part of the tour. Why it intrigued me, I couldn't in that moment tell, but I decided that I would mention it at a more appropriate moment.

We learnt from the lady - whose name, we discovered, was Sylvia - that the curator of the museum, Godfrey, was her father and that he had lived in the house all his life. He had been fascinated by radios from an early age and had been a collector, collecting everything which we saw in the house, and as with any avid collector, he had also developed technical expertise to attempt restoration and repair. His absence for our visit up to that point had not gone unnoticed, but we found that Sylvia seemed pleasant enough company and a knowledgeable guide in her own right, more than capable of deputising for the man himself. At the back of the house, on the first floor, we found a room of shelves full of transistor radios and other devices, and it was clear that the house was not just a place for living in, but also a workplace and, of course, a museum. Whilst you could imagine a train set enthusiast's home literally being taken over by model railways, here vintage radios and televisions were the substitute. The house reminded me of the type of exhibit that you might find at one of those open-air Victorian live museums such as the Black Country Museum or Ironbridge's Blists Hill.

As we looked around at some of the items on display on the shelves, we heard a strange thudding sound. We ignored it at first, but then there was another thud, at which point one of my friends felt that it was an appropriate moment to notify Sylvia of it. In response, Sylvia seemed rather flustered and a little coy on the matter, brushing it off with an unconvincing answer about the noise having been made by the local fox, who liked climbing on the roof. The three of us looked at each other with a knowing suspicion, clearly not believing the answer which had been given, as we knew that the thudding sounds had not come from above, but from below.

Once we had finished touring the upstairs rooms, we made our way downstairs. As we did so, we thought that we heard a man's voice, well-spoken and hollow, sounding as if he were speaking into a muffled microphone and from long ago, calling for something, or someone - although we couldn't make out any of the words – and it seemed to be coming from the living room. As we went past, I decided that I would peer inside, and I am convinced that just as I was about to do so, the televisions flickered once more, and I heard the short sharp crackling sound of static, as if channels were being changed. When I did look inside, I found that the voice had stopped, the television screens were showing vintage footage as before, and that there was clearly no one in the room. Puzzled and unnerved, I continued to follow the others as we went on and walked past the room at the back, which I had spotted earlier.

"Is this room part of the tour?" one of my friends asked. Again, seeming slightly flustered and coy, Sylvia replied in the negative, explaining that it was empty, and again, the three of us looked at each other in the same manner as before, our minds seemingly having decided that the layout of the house pointed to a connection between this room and the strange sounds we had heard whilst upstairs. We headed out into the back garden, through a side door by the kitchen, and I admit, a wry smile came across my face as I saw a kitchen that looked very much like it still entertained the concepts of rationing and 'Dig for Victory'. As we went up a small path towards the back of the garden, I espied an outside toilet, which I pointed out to my friends, and we chuckled, allowing a schoolboy sense of humour to lighten the mood of the afternoon, which had generally taken a somewhat more surreal and alarming direction.

The final part of the tour was of the out-shed - a larger than average sized wooden structure with a metallic roof - and it was here that we saw the centrepiece of the collection: a television from Buckingham Palace. It was a wonderful piece of equipment, and despite being decades old, it was in excellent condition, and had obviously had work done to it, undertaken by a loving hand, that of the curator of course. It was also at this point that Sylvia dropped the bombshell that her father, Godfrey, had recently passed away at the age of 84. It was certainly a bit of a shock, as this had not been mentioned on the website or in any communications. It did, however, explain his absence. Initially, I had thought it strange that we had not been introduced to him, having expected to see him upon entering the living room, sitting in the armchair, surrounded by his beloved vintage television sets. When he had not been present upon our arrival, I theorised that he would most probably have been resting in a bedroom upstairs, whilst Sylvia took us on a tour of the museum, before Godfrey would join us afterwards, but clearly, that was not going to be the case. Seemingly, as a way of compensating for his absence, Sylvia showed us some photographs of Godfrey with his radios, from an album which included images taken from his younger days - I believe that during the War, he had been involved in radar communication – as well as images taken later on in life, as he became something of an expert on radios, and indeed a go-to for the media whenever communication, radio, television etc. were discussed. The most recent image of him had been taken not long before his death and was of him sitting in the armchair in the living room, surrounded by his television sets, with the standing lamp next to the chair and the hardback book on radios upon the small table, just as I had envisaged him.

As we headed back into the house, Sylvia pointed out to us shrapnel damage on the exterior wall, caused by a bomb blast during the Blitz. We also noticed the room next to the kitchen, with a window looking out onto the garden, and I had the impression, that there was something inside which was by the window – what it was, I couldn't in that moment say – but it did cast doubt in my mind about it being empty. Inside, we again heard the voice, but again it stopped with the sound of a short, sharp burst of static just as we entered the living room. Sylvia offered us a cup of tea, which we accepted, and then left, presumably to go and put the kettle on, before walking back, past the living room, and heading upstairs. The three of us looked at each other and discussed our tour, with particular focus being on the strange events which had taken place.

We felt that there was something Sylvia wasn't telling us, something that she didn't want us, as visitors to the museum, to know, and I suggested that it centred upon the room next to the kitchen, the room she had told us was empty, and where I was convinced that the thudding noises had come from. I also felt that it was connected to the television sets in the living room, which had turned on by themselves, as well as the strange voice which had also emanated from the room intermittently. We were very much in two minds about the whole series of occurrences. On the one hand, there was something eminently creepy about the house, as well as an uncomfortable feeling that we would be best served by departing as soon as possible, for our own safety and sanity, fearful of what may be lurking inside the house and whether or not we would be able to escape some uncanny fate; but on the other hand, our sense of curiosity was nagging us to investigate further, our Famous Five or Secret Seven type of adventurism willing us on, the three of us the perfect silly schoolboy types getting into some terrible scrape.

With Sylvia away, our decision was taken, and we made our way out of the living room, crept past the kitchen, and headed for the room behind the closed door. The door, although closed, was not locked, and so we nervously turned the doorknob and went inside.

What we found was not an empty room, but a bedroom. It was warm, humid and musty inside, and clearly in need of fresh air, the windows probably not having been opened for a long, long time. It was a bedroom from a bygone age, very much in keeping with the rest of the house and its 1940s setting, with a large wireless by the side of the bed, looking like it was ready to announce the abdication of the King, the declaration of war, or some such event from that period. Slightly out of place was the DJ deck from the 1970s by the window – it was this that I had seen from outside whilst in the garden – and a collection of vinyl records displayed in a small rack.

It was one of my friends who had seen it first, and they pointed towards the bed, which was to one side of the room, the left-hand side, slightly behind the door. We hadn't paid any great attention to the bed upon entering, being more interested in the presence of the DJ deck, but there was no escaping the fact that there was clearly something there on the bed, lying under the sheets, something long and bulging, something inert. We stood silent for a few moments, stunned and too fearful to speak or move, all the while adrenalin pumped through each of us, as if preparing our bodies for defence against whatever it was that lay before us.

"What is it?" my friends eventually asked. We knew deep down, with a sinking feeling of horror, what it looked like, but it was still a shock when we pulled back the sheets to reveal, lying there, what we immediately recognised to be the 'body' of the old man we had seen in the photographs, the curator of radios. It wasn't, however, a live body as, upon nervously checking, we discovered that there was no pulse or any sign of breathing. It just lay there, as if displayed by a taxidermist, having been preserved after death.

But it was the face which was the most startling thing of all!

Oh, the face!

But...what am I talking about? There was no face!

Where the face should have been, there was nothing but blankness, no eyes, nose, mouth, facial hair...nothing! It was as if the face had departed the body, had been taken away, or been offered to something or somewhere else.

Suddenly there was the sound first of a click, and then of buzzing and humming, the likes of which we had encountered before, that same afternoon. To our amazement, we watched as the 'face' appeared where there had previously been blankness, appearing as if projected onto a television screen from days gone past. And then the 'eyes' opened, then the 'mouth'. We each of us sprung backwards with alarm as, alongside the sudden appearance of its face, the body, automaton, or whatever it was, sparked into life and began to sit up as well! As it did so, a voice emanated from the wireless, and it was his voice, the same voice I had heard before, the same well-spoken and hollow male voice which sounded as if he were speaking into a muffled microphone and from long ago.

"Good afternoon lads, did you enjoy your tour?" it spoke. "I hope Sylvia managed to show you everything which interested you".

This was all too much, and in terror, the three of us ran out of the room, not wanting to stay in that house for a moment longer. Down we went past the living room - where the televisions all now displayed the face of the curator and projected his voice, speaking directly to us - along the hallway, and then out through the front door and into the road. This was no longer some quirky day out or an adventure for a bit of a laugh, this was now a desperate attempt to escape with our sanity, and possibly our lives. As we fled, Sylvia came running downstairs with a look of grave concern, shouting hysterically.

"Godfrey? Godfrey? What's going on? Is everything all right?"

The Windows

Mr Stevens finished work at 6 o'clock and decided to do some early December Christmas shopping. He worked in the West End for a firm that dealt with high-end clients, and as well as being rather well paid, as an added bonus at Christmas, he would usually receive gifts from clients as a thank you for his hard work throughout the year, with some of the clients being particularly generous. A gift which he received pretty much every year was a fine food hamper from the world-famous, celebrated department store, beautifully presented, as you might expect, in a rectangular wicker basket, with the usual cheeses, biscuits, jams, teas etc all inside. As the world-famous shop itself was located just around the corner from his office and was a mere five-minute walk away, he decided - inspired by his own gift - that it would be perfect for his own Christmas shopping. Not only would he be able to find some wonderful high-quality gifts for friends, family, and colleagues, but he would also be able to shop whilst soaking in the most festive of atmospheres that evening, especially with it being a Friday.

Situated on Piccadilly, the store had been established in the early 1700s, with its façade being indicative of the building styles of the time. The red brick and half a dozen rows of sash windows, along with the 18th century-style mechanical clock in the centre - below which is the elegant and visually stunning turquoise entrance with large shop-front windows - convey a grand and timeless welcome to all who visit - to shop, to simply browse, or just to say that they have been there. On arrival, you are in no doubt that it is a department store of luxury, and one that prides itself on tradition, style, and providing a more unique experience than the every-day normality of shopping.

Being close to Christmas, and it also being a Friday evening, there was an excited, expectant atmosphere about Central London. The Christmas lights, of course, added some magic and much needed sparkle to the streets amid the winter darkness of the cold December. Everywhere was buzzing, so much so that Stevens felt glad that he had formed the plan to do some Christmas shopping in this way, rather than taking the much easier and more convenient, but perhaps, more soulless option of just shopping online and having it delivered to home the following day.

Outside the store, standing just to the right of the main entrance, were a group of carol singers collecting for charity, giving an excellent rendition of 'Ding Dong Merrily on High'. It provided a splendid soundtrack as he stared at the window displays showing wonderful things such as a giant Christmas pudding with golden coins pouring out of it; winged mince pies flying over a snowy landscape; and sweets, candies and lollipops which seemed to have come straight from Willy Wonka's factory. Stevens felt, in that moment, that a mug of mulled wine was all that was missing from the festive scene, as the singers moved seamlessly on to another carol as he gazed in amazement at the displays before him.

The magic continued inside as the shop floor was beautifully decorated with large Christmas trees that sparkled effervescently in a variety of colours, with gold and red being predominant. As his eyes surveyed the landscape before him, he noticed that here was a real old-fashioned festive feel to everything that he saw. He imagined himself as a Victorian gentleman in top hat and tails, wearing a splendid frock coat that pretended to keep him warm, and carrying a cane as he walked gracefully and confidently around, browsing the various counters and shelves.

After much deliberation, he finally decided on the chocolates, biscuits, and teas that he would get, making sure that hadn't overlooked anybody who he planned to buy gifts for. He also couldn't help but notice the stall selling candied and marzipan fruits - he loved marzipan fruits and saw them on display in different shapes: bananas, strawberries, apples, corn on the cob, tomatoes, and mushrooms – and moved closer, albeit with a guilty reluctance. As is always the case when you feel the onset of temptation, you try to convince yourself that "it only happens once a year" and that "you only live your life once", despite knowing that you probably shouldn't do what you are inevitably about to and that you will most likely regret it come January. Stevens debated briefly with himself as to whether he should or shouldn't indulge, but despite it facing a stiff battle, the voice of temptation – evident, yet subtle - did claim the victory, and as he was spending a fair amount of money on others, he surmised that he could do so on himself too, and so he decided to treat himself. He asked the member of staff at the counter if he could get a selection box, and he was able to pick out the fruits he wanted, although he found it hard to decide as he was spoilt for choice. As he made his decisions, the lady behind the stall collected the fruits from their individual plate stands, loaded them delicately into the turquoise box and arranged them neatly inside, as if fitting pieces of a jigsaw puzzle together. As the box filled, Stevens subconsciously wondered, greedily, just how many fruits he could get inside the box, although much depended on the weight of it, as this would be how the price would be determined. Eventually, when it became clear that full capacity had been reached, the lady stopped, and then placed a golden ribbon around the box flaps to close it securely with a bow. A label was printed, indicating the weight and the resulting price, and she then handed the box over to him, in the manner of someone handing over an item of the importance of state secrets, a valuable artifact, or an Olympic torch.

"Don't eat them all at once sir" she quipped. At first, Stevens thought the remark a little flippant, but he smiled back at her, treating the remark as her attempt at creating rapport with him.

Before moving on and heading towards the front area of the store to pay, he noticed a wooden advent calendar, with an artist's impression of the store's façade on the front, sitting on one of the stands near to the jams and marmalades section. The advent calendars were being sold on the first floor, along with the rest of the decorations that were for sale, and this was clearly a display version and was around 50cm tall, 40cm wide and 10cm deep. He went over to it, having been impressed by it at first glance, and saw that the impression of the store's façade was indeed a very good one – in fact, it was so good that it almost seemed as if it had been life-like. There was the red brickwork, the mechanical clock, the turquoise entrance area with shop windows either side of the main door, and there too were the rows of sash windows - all just as with the real building itself. The scene the advent calendar portrayed was, naturally, a Christmas one, with festive wreaths and trees also decorating the façade; snow rested on the ground as well as on the roof, whilst shoppers stood outside admiring the window displays of toys and sweets, and from the way the building had been lit, it was clearly late afternoon or early evening. Curious, he opened some of the doors to see what was behind them and found that they hid tiny bags of sweets within the various compartments.

Behind the last of the doors, he found a beige coloured sweet – made from marzipan, he thought - in the shape of what looked like a man. It was a rather strange looking thing and it had about it something that alarmed him as, upon looking at it more closely, Stevens began to doubt that it was supposed to be a man at all, but rather, something else entirely, although he couldn't quite determine what. Of course, he realised that a sweet probably wouldn't have the same level of detail and quality as the artistry of the calendar itself, and he could certainly excuse a sweet for looking more like a caricature when seemingly representing the figure of a man, but this was very different, and was actually quite hideous.

He felt rather uncomfortable and decided that he didn't like it all, especially as he also had the impression that it was staring at him somehow. He quickly closed the door it was hiding behind, wanting not only to keep it away from view, but also to somehow bar its 'escape', before deciding to move on and head for the tills in order to pay.

As he exited the building, the carol singers, who still occupied their spot outside, were now singing 'Good King Wenceslas' and this time, Stevens gave one of the young lads - who couldn't have been any older than 9, and was wrapped up in thick coat, gloves, scarf and bobble hat - some coins for his bucket. The child smiled at him initially, giving a cheery expression of gratitude.

"Thank you very much sir", the lad began in response to the donation, but then followed this, somewhat rather gravely - albeit with an air of innocence - by adding "stay safe, sir". Stevens felt this to be an odd thing to say, quite unlike the usual festive message that accompanied such interactions in the run-up to Christmas. Thinking nothing of it, he smiled nervously back at the lad, turned left onto Piccadilly, rather pleased with himself and his purchases - despite the large dent into his bank account - and walked down towards Green Park tube station. Once inside the station, he made his way down to the Jubilee line platforms, waiting only a couple of minutes for a train to arrive. He boarded, managed to find himself a seat, and sat down, not believing his luck at how quiet the train was for a Friday evening. On the train, he decided to rummage through his turquoise coloured bag to assess his evening's work, and he came across the box of marzipan fruits. He reminded himself that they were his Christmas present to himself, to be opened early on Christmas morning and enjoyed over the festive period, but the temptation was too great. Guiltily, and nervously looking about himself as he did so, he untied the golden bow, opened the box, and sat there, as the train advanced further along the line Eastwards, gorging on one marzipan fruit after another until they had all gone - so delicious were they - wallowing in his own gluttony.

Stevens was at home some 24 hours later when he took in a delivery he had not been expecting. Upon opening the large box, he discovered it to be one of the wooden advent calendars he had seen on the Friday evening. It came with a message attached that simply read 'Merry Christmas'. Stevens contacted all those he could think of who may have sent him such an extraordinary gift, unsure as to who it was from. He knew that the advent calendar was not cheap, and so the generosity of whoever had given it to him was touching and wholly unexpected. He was also acutely aware that he would have to reciprocate the gesture once he knew the identity of the sender.

The advent calendar was almost identical to the one that he had seen in the shop, although there was a difference, and it was this: the addition on his of a small group of carol singers in the scene, standing by the main door. As he examined it, the scene reminded him of how things had been of his own visit to the shop the previous evening, and there was an uncanny likeness in the artistic impression of the carol singers with the real ones he had encountered himself. He thought nothing of it, and simply marvelled at the artistry of the scene before him. He found too, that the advent calendar had been filled with treats. As December had already begun and was progressing nicely, he began to open the doors of the days that had already passed and enjoyed the different sweets they revealed. Jelly babies, wine gums, mini chocolate Santas, jellybeans and a variety of boiled sweets greeted him as the advent calendar offered up its treasures.

As pleased as he was with the gift, there was, lurking at the back of his mind, the image he had of the strange sweet shaped as some sort of 'man' that he had seen in the calendar in the shop. Despite his best attempts at suppression, the advent calendar's arrival, and the opening of the doors to reveal the sweets hidden inside, had revived his thoughts of it. Although he didn't want to explore all the doors in advance, he decided that, to put his mind at ease, he would examine the last one, the 24th, as it was behind this one where the figure had been. He opened it slowly, with a feeling of trepidation, wondering if this door would offer the same reveal as the other calendar had, but thankfully, to his immense relief, he found nothing there but an innocent looking chocolate coin. Smiling to himself - partly with relief, but also with a stern rebuke to himself for being silly - he re-closed the final door, leaving the coin where it was, and then picked the advent calendar up and walked over with it to a mantelpiece in his living room. Here, he placed it in the middle, with a few ornaments and small framed photographs accompanying it on either side, before stepping backwards and then forwards again a couple of times to adjust it accordingly, so that it was perfectly positioned. Having already begun putting up his Christmas decorations, and with the advent calendar now in place and sitting proudly on the mantelpiece, Stevens was content that Christmas was under way.

In its own way, mainly due to its size and location, the advent calendar became the centrepiece of the room, with the beautifully drawn and painted façade of the department store being a wonderful sight. As well as the thought of opening one of the doors each day to see what treat was behind it, Stevens couldn't help but admiring the artistry, but one thing struck him when examining it on the second day, something that he hadn't noticed before. He saw that one of the windows on the façade, where it had previously shown candlelight behind it, now showed nothing but darkness, as if the light in the room behind that particular window had suddenly been extinguished. Stevens initially dismissed it as an oversight on his part, believing himself to have somehow missed it the previous day, but he was also slightly annoyed at what seemed to be an irritating 'artistic fault' in his calendar; however, seeing as it was a gift, and he had already begun to make use of it, he didn't feel it proper to do anything further about it. He also still had no idea where the gift had come from, due to a lack of any response from those who he had contacted upon receiving it, and this would most likely have complicated somewhat any attempt to return it.

After thinking no further about the darkened window for the

rest of that day, he became rather alarmed when, on the following day, another window showed darkness behind it, and a third window showed the same the day after. Next, one of the festive wreaths seen displayed at another of the windows had also changed and now appeared to have completely died. A concern began to grow inside Stevens, as it appeared that some form of transformation was taking place within his advent calendar, and as the days went by more and more changes occurred, the pace at which they did so quickening at an alarming rate. More and more of the windows showed darkness behind them, cobwebs began to appear and then seemed to take over the place, festive greenery continued to die, the clock seemed to come away from the building before falling to the ground, and the brickwork started to crumble too. In essence, there became a general sense of decay about the scene, as if the life within the building was draining away. The shoppers and carol singers seen at the bottom of the scene, outside the building, also seemed to drift away, as if abandoning the place to its seemingly inevitable fate. As the month progressed, a feeling of sadness and despair gradually came over Stevens, seemingly growing with every change which took place. Unable to comprehend what was happening, he found it preposterous that this advent calendar had a scene upon it that was somehow changing before his very eyes - turning from a wonderful festive display into something out of a horror film.

It wasn't just the scene being portrayed which was changing, but also the treats behind the doors as well, as they too deteriorated in quality; indeed, several of the sweets which were revealed to him were inedible, so overcome by mould were they that they would have made him seriously ill had he eaten them. Yet, despite this decay, he found it strangely compelling, as if he somehow had to see what would happen next. A morbid curiosity gripped him, and a voice - the same voice inside him that had been pushing him with temptation thus far – was telling him to accept what was happening and allow himself to be shown whatever it was that was being laid out before him.

About a week before Christmas, there came another change. This time a man had appeared at one of the windows, and upon further inspection, Stevens believed him to be middle-aged and wearing a periwig and the attire of a gentleman of the 18th century. From his rather portly look as well as his jolly manner, it seemed that he had succumbed to gluttony and had been gorging himself, most probably on Christmas treats. Compared to the other changes to the advent calendar that had taken place, Stevens found this more agreeable, and he could certainly imagine a gentleman such as this celebrating the festive season 300 years ago in a building such as was being shown. The portly gentleman was still there the following day, but this time, Stevens noticed that at the window directly to the left of him (from Stevens' point of view), a shape had appeared, subtly emerging from the darkness, indistinct and with a pale hue, but seemingly directing its attention towards the man.

On examining the scene again, the next day, Stevens saw that the shape had gone from the window at which it had been previously. Instead, what he now saw sent shivers right through his entire body: the portly gentleman was still there at his window, but the shape he had seen the previous day had moved and now appeared directly behind the man, this time as a more distinct figure and expertly illustrated. Stevens recognised this new figure instantly, as it looked exactly like the odd-looking sweet that had been behind the last door of the advent calendar in the shop. Its skin appeared smooth and greasy, with a beige-yellow colour to it, and it certainly didn't seem to be human in the sense of what we may consider as being human. From its manner, it was undoubtedly malevolent, and Stevens realised that the man was in perilous danger. In horror, he shouted to him, warning him to beware the thing lurking behind him, although he realised, of course, that it was pointless as the man would not be able to hear him. Despite knowing deep down that he was being silly for shouting at an illustration on an advent calendar, Stevens had become so attached to the scene and the changes taking place within it, that this new development was too much for him to bear.

He pondered the man's plight, trying desperately to think of a way by which he could be saved, before eventually realising that there was nothing that could be done. He decided that if there was to be some terrible atrocity committed within the scene, which he had no control over, he simply did not want to witness it. He threatened to destroy the advent calendar, thinking that it would be the best course of action for his own sanity. However, as he went to pick it up and dispose of it, the voice inside him came to him once again, urging him to refrain from doing so, and although it went against his better judgement, he eventually convinced himself that destroying the advent calendar would be unnecessary. Unable to bring himself to destroy it, and with no other obvious course of action, he turned it around so that it faced the wall, a feeling of guilt rising inside him as he feared that he too was abandoning both the place and the portly gentleman to their fate.

For the next few days Stevens did all he could to avoid the advent calendar as it sat there, facing towards the wall, as if in disgrace. He felt helpless, as he still pondered, not only over what was to be done, but also as to the fate of the portly gentleman at the window, unable to find a suitable solution. On several occasions, he dared himself to turn the advent calendar around and see how the scene had progressed since the last time, out of morbid curiosity, but then decided against it. Eventually, however, he found that he could not escape the scene on the front of the advent calendar forever as, on Christmas Eve morning, he found that somehow, despite not touching it since turning it around, it was no longer facing the wall, but towards him again. He now felt as though he were being teased or mocked by some unknown force that had seemingly taken possession of the advent calendar, and he decided that this time he would destroy it.

As he picked it up, he noticed, with great surprise, that the advent calendar was now as he had first taken possession of it, with the façade of the shop back to normal, looking as gloriously festive and full of life and joy as it had been right at the start. The festive greenery was lush, the brickwork was in impeccable condition, the clock was back in its rightful place, and the revellers had also returned. In addition, he saw that the portly gentleman and, perhaps more importantly, the strange, malevolent figure, had both disappeared, with there being no darkness or shadow for anything to be lurking in.

Stevens felt hugely relieved by these developments, believing that what he had been witness to over the recent weeks had been some extraordinary trick played upon himself by his own imagination. Thankful that he seemed to have his advent calendar back the way he wanted it and the way it should have been all along, he decided to open the remaining doors, gorging himself on the sweets within. The sweets were of the most excellent quality, and he enjoyed them as much as he had the others, although it is probably fair to suggest that out of all the sweets he had devoured, the marzipan fruits - which he had bought as a treat for himself and had eaten so soon after purchase – were still his favourites.

As he came to the door for the 24th, however, a hesitation, brought about by a sudden fear, came over him once again. Despite the fact that, on the previous occasion he had opened this door and found nothing but a chocolate coin, he was acutely aware that it had been behind the 24th door on the advent calendar in the shop where he had first seen the strange figure - albeit then as a sweet – which had subsequently appeared in the distressing scenes he had recently been a witness to. The door, he noticed, seemed to be slightly ajar, as if it had recently been opened, although Stevens knew that he himself had not been the one who had opened it. Again, debate raged within him as to whether he should open the door or ignore it. Although rational thinking had it that a chocolate coin would be revealed, as it had been upon previously checking, after all that he believed he had seen over recent days, he was becoming gripped by a growing feeling of dread that it would instead be the strange figure, in sweet form, that he would see. That voice within him which had been communicating to him throughout, egging him on, spoke to him once again and urged him to open it. Slowly, and trembling with fear, he moved his hand to open the little door. As it opened, he felt the dread dissipate from him, replaced by a sense of relief, as thankfully, he realised that there was no reason to fear what was lurking in the tiny compartment behind the door, as it was empty. There was no strange figure inside, and in fact, there were no sweets at all. Of course, after the initial relief at the compartment being empty, his mood changed to that of disappointment and surprise at there being no sweets at all for him on that final day of the countdown. Although he wondered what had become of the chocolate coin, he knew, that over the next few days, he would have plenty more wonderful food to enjoy anyway, and so, placated, he placed his advent calendar back on the mantelpiece, facing outwards once again, feeling hopeful and excited for the first time in weeks, and began his final Christmas preparations.

As an epilogue, it should be relayed to you that the police were called to Stevens' house at around 4 o'clock that very afternoon after reports that heavy and sickening screams were heard by someone who had been walking past. Inside the house, the police found Stevens lying on the floor, dead, with a look of extreme terror on his face, although there was apparently no sign of any physical injury, or of forced entry. A strong, persistent smell of almonds was also apparently present inside the house, while the living room showed evidence of a struggle, with objects seemingly having been thrown about, possibly at something that had been there with him inside the room. A statement from the passer-by who had alerted the police suggested that when walking past the house, they had seen Stevens appearing at his living room window, which overlooked the road that passes it. Standing behind him was, the passer-by said, 'some beast, probably not of human origin, its manner horrible and its intent clearly one of pure evil'. At first, they thought they had imagined it, but moments later, after walking onwards for a further 50m, they heard the screaming and knew that some horrible event had taken place, at which point they called 999.

There is probably no need for me to expand further upon the description of this fiend which was seen at the window with Stevens, as you have almost certainly already visualised it for yourself, using what you have already read above. It is also likely that the fate of the portly gentleman, who Stevens had observed in his advent calendar, can also be guessed at with some confidence, too. In fact, it may be worthwhile searching the records for any reports of similarly described gentlemen dying of fright on Christmas Eve in London during the 18th century. It would certainly be remarkable if there were indeed such records, and it would be hoped that eyewitness accounts would also exist, in the event that they may bear similarities with that for the death of Stevens.

As for the advent calendar itself, no explanation as to who had given it to Stevens as a gift can be offered. As it was found sitting quite peacefully on the mantelpiece in the living room, the police attached no importance to it during their investigation, although perhaps this was a mistake as, despite it appearing to be a thing of festive beauty, it may not have been harmless. It seems that contained within it was a warning to the gluttonous.

The Student House

Perhaps the first moment in which alarm bells should have begun to ring was immediately upon arrival, and the discovery of a significant pile of mail lying on the mat just inside the front door. It was an overwhelming discovery, made even more startling by the fact that a number of the envelopes were marked with the words 'FINAL NOTICE' in the most alerting of red coloured print. What these letters were became obvious upon further examination: gas bills, electricity bills, water bills, phone and internet bills - and they were not just bills, but repeated demands for payments, and then warnings of the consequences of payment not being received within x amount of days. As a first impression, it was, quite frankly dreadful, and would have left anyone entering 10 Gooden Road with several questions requiring answers of the utmost urgency. What had happened to the previous tenants? Why had they vacated the property, seemingly in a hurry, and left the accounts in such a state? And, what was to be done by the new tenants – would they be required to sort out the mess they had inherited from their predecessors?

Hindsight, being the wonderful thing that it is, would have told anyone entering the property as new tenants, that the best course of action upon arrival, would have been to depart as quickly as possible, never to return. Additionally it would have been stressed upon them of the need to cancel any contract they had with the property, and find another abode elsewhere, ensuring that they had no further dealings with or thoughts of the place of any kind.

10 Gooden Road was a small, unassuming and unremarkable late 1950s to early 1960s terraced house, with an untidy front garden - whose only features of note were weeds, a rusted front gate, an unattractive concrete path leading to the bland front porch, and a dustbin – which was quite befitting its status as a student rental house. Inside, the house was just as uninspiring, and although not unclean, as such, certainly gave a feeling of having been a little neglected. The carpets, for example, looked as though they needed a vacuum cleaner put to them with some urgency; the walls were mostly a dirty beige colour and were stained in places, while patches of mould could also be seen dotted about, especially near the ceiling; and there was also a subtle, but unpleasant, dampness and mustiness about the place too. The layout of the house was nothing out of the ordinary: to the right, upon entering, was a small space which could be generously labelled as a reception area, but was in reality a place to store anything that couldn't be found a home for elsewhere; facing it was a small narrow kitchen with all the usual appliances; on the opposite side was a living room with a ground floor bedroom adjoining, which looked out onto the back garden; and in between kitchen and living room was a staircase which led to the first floor. Upstairs, there were three further small bedrooms and, in the far right-hand corner a bathroom. The back garden could be reached from the kitchen or through a set of patio doors in the ground floor bedroom, and was slightly more attractive than the front, with a better-kept lawn, small selection of flowers and standard garden furniture.

The estate where the house was located, Hades Place, was not a terribly inspiring area either, and could be described as rather grim. If you were to happen upon it and decided to explore, you might determine that it had built up during that mid 20th century period – and although its appearance certainly lended itself to that theory, its history dated back much further, as will be highlighted in due course. At a fork in the main road, which ran down to the estate, there was a small corner shop - a mere 60 seconds walk from the student house - outside which was a public payphone. Beyond the store, along the right-hand fork, was a line of houses - which were as big and splendid, as the houses on the estate were small and unattractive - with the road leading down towards a primary school and then a line of shops and a small pub, The Old Bethanie.

But whilst the area was not one where anyone would perhaps wish to stay beyond university years, and the house itself was not terribly appealing either, it could be argued that home is whatever one makes it. With this in mind, it is no surprise that the students decided that Hades Place and 10 Gooden Road fulfilled their requirements, as the positive attributes seemed to outweigh all else. The estate was an ideal location, being within walking distance of the city centre, local supermarket, and university campus; and it was also very affordable, which was probably of most importance to them. Also, with competition for housing among the student population being as fierce as it was, 10 Gooden Road, despite its faults, was seen, in the world of student accommodation as something of a prize, and would never have any trouble being snapped-up.

Seb was a history student who had been in need of new housemates for his second year, having not bonded terribly well with those who he been grouped with in on-campus accommodation during his first. He had found an online post on the university's student accommodation forum, advertising the need for an extra person to join a trio who had already found somewhere to live. He responded to the post, as he had with others in the past, and whilst none of those had come to anything beyond initial house visits, he was rather more hopeful of this latest one. His communication with the author of the advert seemed far more promising, and they agreed to meet up over a drink for further discussions, where again, his optimism increased as he found the tall and lanky politics student Clay, to be more to his liking than the other students who he had been involved with when searching for accommodation thus far. Unfortunately, they were unable to arrange a house visit, although Clay was able to provide photographs of the house to a satisfactory extent instead, and with time becoming rather pressing, Seb decided that it was important that new accommodation was arranged as soon as possible, and that subject to the others' approval, he would be happy to take up the offer of a room. Seb was invited to meet the rest of the group a week later, and was introduced to Miya, a stocky Brummie studying sociology, and Sofi, a pony-tailed studious girl from Germany, who like Clay was studying politics. They all seemed to get along rather well, and it was agreed that Seb would join them to complete their group of four. The necessary paperwork was then completed and contracts signed over the summer, ahead of a September moving-in date.

It was Seb who discovered the mass of unopened mail, as described at the beginning of this narrative, lying on the doormat. As the member of the group who had chosen to take on responsibility for all of the bills (the costs would be divided between the four of them, but he would be the one arranging payment and dealing with correspondence) it was he who contacted all of the companies supplying services to the property. Following dialogue with each of them, the debts were all settled, and the accounts transferred over to them as the new tenants, although the further details of this process are not of interest here.

Away from the massive headache caused by the final notices, the four students settled into their accommodation nicely, and despite the unappealing characteristics described earlier, made themselves rather comfortable, finding that their new home suited their needs. The house wasn't without its quirks, however:

the smoke detector in the kitchen, for example, was exceptionally sensitive, and would activate at the slightest hint of heat in the kitchen area, even in the event of one of the students simply boiling water; the power shower was another appliance that displayed exaggerated and temperamental behaviour, producing the most horrific of screeching noises when in use, although only late at night; while the central heating system had a tendency to flippantly turn itself on at random intervals in warm weather and then switch itself off during cold.

At first, these quirks were not taken terribly seriously, the students theorising that with this being a rented student property, the appliances in the house were more likely to be temperamental anyway, but over time, their attitude began to change as new problems arose, with a greater intensity than before. The first of these involved the washing machine, which began to leak – producing not just a trickle of water underneath it, but a full-scale continuous flood – even when not in use. This was then followed a day later by a problem with the freezer section of the fridge-freezer, which began to ice-up to such an extreme that, despite everything they tried in order to address the problem, the ice just kept on building and expanding, until eventually they were unable to close the freezer door. Next, whilst Sofi was cooking in the kitchen one afternoon, lumps of plaster began to fall from the ceiling without warning, dropping indiscriminately throughout the cooking area, not only ruining her cooking, but also causing her some cuts and bruises.

As these problems continued to arise, the students began to ponder the fantastical notion that 10 Gooden Road was a house that seemed somehow cursed. These problems were not just, it seemed, regular faults which could be dealt with via a minimum of fuss, but were major issues which required more specialised attention, and were also both rather numerous – too numerous to be coincidental – and extraordinarily odd in their manner. Eventually, they felt that it had become necessary to alert the landlord of the property to the problems, in the expectation that they would be provided with some assistance. Remarkably, their complaints were pre-empted, in what would prove to be a further escalation in the utter bizarreness of the situation in which they increasingly found themselves to be.

It was on the morning which the students took the decision to contact the landlord, that there was a knock at their front door. It was a strange sounding knock, as it was the sound of a knocking made by an iron door knocker attached to a door made of wood - quite out of keeping with how a knock at their door should have been, bearing in mind that their front door was modern and of glass and metal, and had no door knocker of any kind. Seb, believing it to have been a delivery for the house, made his way, in a rather blasé manner, to the front door and opened it without a second thought. What awaited him as he opened the door, provided quite a shock as, standing there, outside the front door of 10 Gooden Road, was not a courier, but two visitors. They were a man and a woman, both smartly attired, but a rather odd couple he thought, with a manner about them which suggested that they were the type of people who lacked what could be termed 'people skills'. Anyone who has worked in a customer service environment, especially as a contractor, will have, at some point, worked with difficult-to-please directors and clients who know nothing of front of house day-to-day operations, but observe them with a slyness, speaking little but watching everything like a spy, always with a critical eye and then speaking ill of them behind their back – and this odd couple standing outside 10 Gooden Road certainly gave the impression that they were of similar ilk. Seb felt that they seemed unwilling to speak unless absolutely necessary, whilst their facial expressions seemed cold, distant, vacant, and full of contempt, as if they would not look at you, but through you - if, that is, they felt the need to look in your direction at all. He was taken aback by them, but offered a friendly, if nervous greeting, and enquired of their business.

"I am Mr Monton, and this is Ms Aven" the man replied robotically - his voice raspy - with a chilling coldness, adding, without looking at Seb "we represent the landlord of this property, and we are here to investigate the problems which you have been ex-periencing". The others had joined Seb and they were all amazed at this new development, seeing as they had not yet reported the problems to the landlord, but before any of them could respond, the odd couple were both stepping across the threshold and into the house. As they did so, a subtle change in both their man-ner could be detected, as smug, almost self-congratulatory smiles flirted across their faces.

Once inside the front area, Seb covertly made a closer inspec-tion of the odd couple who represented their landlord. Both were paler than what would be deemed normal, he thought, and their skin rather dry (if not parched), and paper-like in texture; their eyes seemed hollow and without life or soul to them, as if they were not real eyes at all, and not once did he see either visitor blink; and as for their mouths, Seb saw that whereas with most people there would be a moistness thanks to the presence of sal-iva, with both of them there was nothing. He was also struck by their hair as, for both of them, it seemed excessively matted, and he was sure that he detected 'movement' therein, as if the hair were some kind of habitat for tiny crawling creatures. None of the students said anything to either of the visitors, beyond re-marks surrounding the issues they were having, but Seb certainly felt rather uncomfortable being in their presence as they made their inspection of the various faults. The temperature had also dropped noticeably, and there was now a stillness in the air, as if the oxygen within the house was gradually being sucked away, with an oppressiveness seeming to take over.

The odd couple seemed to know, without being told, what the problems were, as if they were either dealing with recurrent issues or - Seb wondered, subconsciously attempting to dismiss his own suspicion as ridiculous – they somehow had had a hand in their inception. They were accompanied, as they moved about, not by the usual smells you might associate with such agents, such as an appealing perfume, deodorant or aftershave, but by a strange earthy smell, requiring windows around the house to be opened for ventilation and fumigation afterwards, despite it being the colder part of the year. Also, as the students followed them as they went around the house, all four felt their scalps becoming itchy, as if their hair had become ridden with lice or similar creatures.

Although the visit was not a terribly lengthy one, for the students it felt like an eternity - as is often the case in uncomfortable situations where you wish for a rapid conclusion - but to their credit, the odd couple performed a thorough and detailed inspection, and upon their departure promised that the issues would be promptly addressed. After they had gone Sofi resolved to peer surreptitiously through the front room curtains to watch the visitors further, although she found that she could see no indication of their presence outside at all, not even as they would have walked away. The four of them discussed the latest developments, and all agreed that the experience had been surreal and rather unnerving, with Miya thinking the visitors to have been quite creepy, coming across rather like, she said, 'a pair of demonic lieutenants'.

The odd couple kept to their word, and the problems were addressed speedily and efficiently as promised, with workmen being assigned to the various jobs, and the faults resolved. For about a month, it seemed that the students were able to carry on living in their house comfortably, and could put the initial problems behind them. But then, something quite alarming happened, which seemed not only to bring about a new phase of their problems, but to elevate them to a higher, much more frightening level.

One morning, with the others having already departed for early lectures, Sofi awoke to find herself the last person in the house. Although it was quiet, with the others having gone, the house still seemed 'lively' somehow. She thought it rather curious, and so she got out of bed, put her slippers and dressing gown on, and opened her bedroom door, but as she did so, she was met by a huge swarm of flies (it was like being confronted, she later said, by one of the plagues of Egypt). She screamed in horror as they flew about her, in what seemed like their hundreds, as if undertaking some form of attack. She flailed her arms wildly in a desperate attempt to disperse them, but it soon became clear that it was futile, as the house was full of flies, and not only that, but that an over-powering stench of death also permeated throughout.

It was awful, and as she tried to compose herself, she held one hand to her face to cover her nose and mouth, and waved the other to fend off the flies, but despite this, they just kept on coming, like a swarm of locusts all streaming in from the most terrible of places. She knew that she had to do something about it quickly, and so, with great haste, she set about opening all the windows and using an anti-insect repellent to try and get rid of them. To her relief, as she went about the house, she could find no person or animal dead inside; and suspecting the air vent in the bathroom to be the entry point for the flies, she also inspected that, but discovered it to be clear, adding to the mystery of the episode.

Throughout the vast majority of the house, her method of getting rid of the flies eventually proved to be sufficient, but she noticed that it would be more of a challenge in the downstairs bedroom, where the problem appeared to have been greater. It seemed that the flies were rather attracted to one of the windows in particular, settling there as if it were some kind of hive for them, refusing to leave when the opportunity arose. Sofi determined that more rigorous action was required here and, after a great effort and also notable length of time that morning, the flies were finally expelled, whilst the use of an air freshener, soon took care of the awful smell of death, allowing the house to return to some sort of normality. She decided to report the incident, and the house was subsequently given an inspection by a pest controller, whilst the vent was also properly examined, in case a dead pigeon or some other bird had become lodged in it. But, despite the investigations, no cause for the appearance of the flies or indeed the foul stench was established, and there was thankfully, no further occurrence of either problem.

In addition to the above, Clay also had an uncanny episode one afternoon whilst returning home from campus. It was a clear day and mild for the time of year, and so he decided to take a slightly longer route back to 10 Gooden Road. The walk was, to begin with, uneventful, taking him downwards from the main campus and then on a meandering wooded path towards Hades Place. It was as he emerged from the footpath into the estate that he suddenly felt a significant drop in temperature. He shivered, not wholly because of the cold, but also because of an uneasiness brought about, it seemed, by his location. He quickened his walking pace, endeavouring to reach home as soon as possible, but in passing the corner shop, he noticed, in the far corner of his eye, two figures, loitering outside, in the manner of those staking-out a certain location. There was something familiar about them, but also an unpleasantness too, and he decided that it was best to ignore them and continue towards home as quickly as possible.

Unfortunately, the temperature did not improve once he was indoors, and in fact it seemed to get even colder. The heating had once again switched off, but the impression he had was that, not only was the cold he felt emanating from inside the house, but the source of it was the kitchen as, upon entering, he found it was of the greatest intensity there. He saw that the freezer was in a terrible state as it had frozen over once again, but this time to such an extent that the ice had broken out and was enveloping the outside of the appliance as well as the inside, and also appeared to be 'growing'. It was an awful sight, and to Clay, it seemed that he had stepped into some arctic world, with the ice being somehow alive and creeping outwards, expanding with an ominous slyness to it. He panicked, unsure of what to do, but as he stepped away, with his hands to his head in astonishment, he saw, staring at him through the kitchen window from outside in the back garden, the odd couple who had visited on behalf of the landlord, and who, he realised, had been standing outside the corner shop that very afternoon. He yelped with horror. He was rooted to the spot, and it seemed that he too was now being enveloped by the ice from the freezer, as he saw it cascading across the floor and then frosting over him with terrifying speed, and he could feel the cold burrowing deep into his body, as if transforming him into some kind of Jack Frost-like creature. All the while, the odd couple seemed to watch with a terrible delight. Miya, arrived home just then, and upon hearing Clay's distress, rushed into the kitchen, and saw him there in a state of hysteria. But she found that there was no ice outside the fridge-freezer or on Clay's person, and despite his insistence of being watched from outside, there was nobody there.

The continuous barrage of strange events, which seemed to become more alarming, more distressing as time progressed, began to weigh heavily upon the students, their mood gradually darkening and their determination to stick-it out, as it were, receding.

Seb, by his own volition – inspired by the theories of their house being somehow cursed - had begun researching the history of the local area, and in particular, Hades Place. Unfortunately, much of what he found was rather dry and of no interest to this narrative, but he did find a piece in a rather obscure book in the university library, which told of a Mr Hanseyn, who had resided on the site in the 16th century. According to the passages in the book, this Mr Hanseyn was a curious fellow who suffered from a skin ailment which sounded to Seb as rather like a severe form of eczema. Little was actually known about him which could be shared with certainty, but it was rumoured that he was a performer of dark arts and sorcery, preying on unsuspecting residents in the local area and those travelling through, conducting strange experiments on them - the details of which were unknown, but likely utterly appalling. Apparently, he was accompanied by two 'others', a man and a woman – rumoured to be siblings – who were not local and were both nameless. Their exact relationship to Mr Hanseyn was never discovered, although it was suggested that they assisted him in his experiments, possibly acting as his 'lieutenants', and it was added that, as well as being assistants to him, they may even have been his earliest subjects.

The book speculated that Mr Hanseyn's 'reign of evil' lasted several months, before eventually, the local authorities were informed of his activities and decided to act against him. However, upon arrival at his abode in their attempt to arrest him one morning, he was nowhere to be found, with the house appearing as if it had been abandoned on the instant. According to witnesses, one of the local men had been keeping watch on the house prior to the authorities' arrival, and was adamant that Mr Hanseyn had been inside the whole time, not exiting at any moment. The house was thoroughly searched, but no trace of him could be found, and it was as if he had simply vanished into thin air. As for the other two, they were found half a mile away, both swinging from the branches of the same tree, and seemingly quite dead. They were buried in the grounds of the nearby church in anonymous graves, but locals would later describe the place as 'restless', with some indicating that they had seen an 'odd couple' lingering in the vicinity.

Mr Hanseyn was never seen again – there were certainly no recorded sightings of him, anyhow – but in the months and years that followed his disappearance, many spoke of having strange experiences whilst in the locale (which would later be named Hades Place), with people telling of feeling a 'presence' there, as well as hearing a scratching sound, as if someone were scraping long fingernails onto the palms of their hands in order to scratch vigorously.

Seb found the stories surrounding Mr Hanseyn to be intriguing, although with there being little in the way of evidence to back-up what was said, or any mention of him elsewhere, he thought it to be little more than a local folk tale which had no real relevance, despite suiting the curse theory. He did, however, allow himself a wry smile, thinking that Mr Hanseyn's assistants reminded him of the strange Mr Monton and Ms Aven who had visited the students previously.

It was about this time that another, rather curious problem arose. There was a storm one night, with heavy rain and significant gusts of wind, and Seb, not being a great sleeper at the best of times, found it to be a restless night, although it was not necessarily the storm itself which kept him awake. He noticed that one of the full-length windows which looked out into the back garden from his room on the ground floor was shaking quite noticeably, causing disturbance. Assuming it to be as a result of the wind, he thought it to be no more than an irritant that would pass when the wind eased, and did his best to ignore it, as he tried, albeit in vain, to sleep. However, on the following day the window shook once more, and again on the next, shaking violently, as if it was still being buffeted by strong winds, despite the air being calm and still. Upon further inspection, Seb found that the window glass had become loose within its fittings, most likely, he thought, due to a combination of age, stress and poor maintenance, with the storm probably having had an impact on it as well. It was clearly yet another problem which needed to be addressed, and by now, Seb was becoming rather tired of them, and no doubt, he thought, so too was the landlord.

With regards to the landlord, Seb noted that the four of them had never had any direct correspondence or interaction with them, whoever they were. In fact, when he thought about it further, he realised that they knew nothing at all about their landlord either, with everything going through his representatives, the odd couple.

Also, whereas before he had reported a problem not only with a determination that he wanted it to be addressed, but with a confidence that he knew it would be, this time Seb felt anxious about doing so without knowing why - somewhere in back of his mind there was a reluctance and a nagging feeling that it would perhaps be best not to report this particular problem, but leave it be. His anxiety was heightened somewhat by a comment made by one of Miya's classmates, a mature student named Glen, who popped round one afternoon and noticed the window shaking whilst he was out in the garden smoking a cigarette.

"If it were the bars of a cage rattling like that window is" Glen remarked, with Seb in earshot, "you would reckon something were trying to get out", without expanding further on what he meant by it, and Seb, not wanting to come across as worried, didn't press him for more, either. Nevertheless, eventually, despite his concerns, report the problem Seb did, and he received a very hasty and enthusiastic – suspiciously so he thought – response from Mr Monton that an engineer would be sent to 10 Gooden Road forthwith.

A workman was dispatched promptly, arriving at 10 Gooden Road a day after Mr Monton's response. He examined the window and confirmed that whilst the frame was perfectly fine, it was the glass which had, for some reason, become loose, and would need to be replaced. Seb noted that the workman indicated this was not the first time it had happened, and thought it curious, but naturally was more concerned about the work being done and this latest problem being resolved. The workman measured up the window, and whilst he did so, Seb offered him a cup of tea, before heading out of the room and round to the kitchen to make it. When he returned, he found that the pane of glass from the window had been removed and was standing up against the wall, to one side of the room. It was a large pane of glass, as the window was tall - about the height of a slightly taller than average person - and it was clearly worn around the edges.

All four of the students were at home that morning, and by now, the others had joined Seb to view the progress of the work thus far, with Sofi remarking that it was the same window as had attracted the flies during her encounter with them. It was at this juncture that the workman informed them that he needed to return to his van parked around the corner – presumably to get some tools and possibly a new pane of glass - but would return presently. Clay escorted the workman to the door before returning to the room, whilst Miya went to the kitchen to make herself a drink, leaving Seb, Sofi and Clay chatting in the room, perfectly content with the innocuous pane of glass propped up against the wall.

Moments after Miya's departure, Sofi noticed that the pane of glass had suddenly gained a 'vibration' to it, and so the three of them stopped talking and observed. As they stood there, they viewed the glass with astonishment as it began to shake, all by itself – gently to begin with, but then gradually with an increasingly greater ferocity.

"Oh my god, it's shaking!" Miya heard Sofi cry out whilst she was in the kitchen, waiting for the kettle to boil.

"Is everything ok?" she shouted back, before hearing further cries, both of which also came from Sofi and were presumably directed at Clay and Seb.

"Do something!" and then "Stop it!"

Miya detected hysteria in Sofi's voice and she knew that something was wrong. A loud thudding noise was the next thing she heard, also emanating from the ground floor bedroom, and at this she stopped what she was doing and made her way back to the room, but as she did so, there was a terrible scream, and she saw Seb and Sofi, both with a look on horror and panic on their faces, leap forward in the direction of the pane of glass that had been propped up against the wall. Miya then ran forwards, but before she could enter the room to see what had happened, the door slammed shut before her, barring her entry. She banged on the door, shouting, pleading to be allowed in and demanding to know what was going on. Sofi answered, trying desperately to open the door for her, but found that she could not. Miya could tell from her voice that Sofi was in tears and that something truly terrible and incomprehensible was taking place before her very eyes. Miya again pleaded with her to tell her what was happening, and Sofi, panting with sheer panic as she did so, described - albeit in a rather broken fashion - something so horrible, that Miya shook as she listened:

As the glass had begun to shake, Clay had moved closer to take a look at it, but had started when the three of them saw a hand - red, dry and itchy in appearance, with skin flaking significantly - suddenly appear, slowly feeling its way out, from inside the side of the pane of glass! The fingers clawed their way outwards, gradually revealing themselves in horrifying fashion, and the nails - which were long, incredibly old and manky - at first tapped on the glass, but then started to scratch at the back of a second hand which also then appeared, producing a nasty scraping sound infinitely worse than that of nails on a chalkboard. And then, the rest of the arms appeared, followed by a leg. Next, the beginnings of a torso and head emerged, and then a second leg, and suddenly, before they could react sufficiently to what was happening, another being, vulgarly human-like and totally malevolent, had fully emerged and was there with them inside the room. It grabbed Clay, gripping him tightly with its hideous hands, and began to pull at him. Seb ran over to help him, and it was at this point that Sofi had screamed.

From outside the room, Miya felt helpless. She could hear every second of what was happening but could see nothing. Sofi was crying and rambling in her words, and Miya knew that she was clearly in shock.

"HELP! LET GO!" came a yell, full of terror. From the commotion that Miya could hear, there was clearly a struggle going on inside the room. Sofi now left the door, which still refused to open, and Miya determined that she simply had to gain entry, whichever way she could. Remembering that she could reach the room from the back garden, she went back to the kitchen, found the key to the back door, unlocked and opened it, and then hurried round to the bedroom. When she got there, it became clear to her that Seb and Sofi had been locked in a battle of tug of war over Clay, against a foe who was trying to pull him away. Unfortunately, at the very moment of Miya's arrival, they were defeated as they were simply unable to cling on to him any longer, with their opponent proving to be too strong. Miya saw, very briefly, this thing – some kind of man, but with the most awful skin – with Clay held in its clutches, dragging him back with it to where it had come from, from inside the side of the pane of glass!

Everything happened so fast, and as the three remaining students stood there inside the room, in stunned silence - all devastated by the extraordinary and horrific turn of events - with the pane of glass now lying inert and propped up against the wall as before, Seb remembered something he had read about Mr Hanseyn whilst undertaking research into the local area. The following words from the obscure book in the university library came to him, bringing a feeling of utter horror: "*at the time, it was suggested by some that he had hidden himself in plain sight*".

There was a knocking at the front door just then, and it was the workman standing outside, waiting to re-enter the house. Also standing outside the house, behind the workman, but on the opposite side of the road, was the odd couple, silently observing 10 Gooden Road, with celebratory smirks on both of their faces.

As an anecdote to add to the above narrative, I must say that, when looking into the side of a pane of glass once before, I myself noticed that it appeared to resemble some kind of 'other world', having a remarkable striped green complexion to it, and thought the sight to be reminiscent of something out of The Matrix films. It was certainly a rather curious effect, and in conjunction with the events at 10 Gooden Road (if we accept them as having actually happened), did prompt the rumination as to whether a being could hide therein, using the inside of the side of a pane of glass as an abode and as somewhere to conduct their foul deeds, only emerging when necessary, to find a new place to hide, or to prey on the unsuspecting.

With regards to the pane of glass from 10 Gooden Road, one wonders if should have been smashed to pieces, never to be used again, rather than remaining intact and used as evidence in a missing persons case by the police, who for all intents and purposes, were rather sceptical and disbelieving of the story. Such action would, of course, have provided a quite appalling dilemma, as the poor unfortunate Clay would probably have been lost forever as a result - although it could be argued that was his fate anyway – but smashing the glass may have been a necessary evil in order to deny Mr Hanseyn (if it were he) the opportunity of escaping once again, assuming, of course, that he hadn't already done so and hidden elsewhere, undetected.

Sometime later, a group of four students entered 10 Gooden Road, having recently completed the necessary paperwork and signed contracts to begin renting the property for the rest of the academic year and then beyond. Unaware of any of the events mentioned above, they thought it a stroke of good fortune that the house had become available when it had, as all four of them were new to the area having previously been elsewhere, and had been in search of somewhere new to live. They were informed that the previous tenants had vacated the property early into their contract - for reasons which were not made known - and that after a brief time, the property had then been put back on the market. When they arrived at the property for the first time, the students found that lying on the floor inside the front door, was a pile of envelopes, many of which were marked with the words 'FINAL NOTICE' in the most alerting of red coloured print.

About The Author

Stephen Rawlinson

Stephen lives in London and has been writing ghost stories since 2009.

He is a former Scout Leader, and his experiences helped inspire some of his stories. These first appeared in the Scout troop newsletter, which he edited for over a decade.

Stephen has a Bachelor of Arts in History, and his love and fascination for the past has played a significant part of his stories, whilst places where he has either worked at or visited, have also provided inspiration.

His love of ghost stories, primarily those of M. R. James, but also of other writers as well, helped to ignite his desire to create his own tales.

He is a non-professional photographer, focusing primarily on landscapes, architecture and travel, and he also enjoys exploring London and hiking in the countryside.